House
of Special
Purpose

House of Special Purpose

ISBN: 978-1-7348524-8-6 (hardback)
         978-1-7348524-2-4 (paperback)
         978-1-7348524-1-7 (ebook)

Printed in the United States of America

House
of Special
Purpose

A Jeannie Loomis Novel

GARY J. ROSE

ALSO, BY GARY J. ROSE

Jeannie Loomis Novels

Ark of the Covenant – Raid on the Church of
Our Lady Mary of Zion

Star Chamber

Forgotten Plans

Non-fiction

Towards the Integration of Police Psychology
Techniques to Combat

Juvenile Delinquency in K-12 Classrooms.

Hitting Rock Bottom

How to Create a Public-School Military Academy

Teaching Inside the Walls

I am fortunate as a writer to be surrounded by a great support group of relatives and friends, who unknowingly, in each of their various ways, help me through those long months needed to complete a novel. Without their help, this book would not be possible.

Special thanks to Mike and Mary Lake and my mother for volunteering the many hours needed to read the rough draft of my manuscript, making valuable suggestions while doing so. And, to my cousins, Drs. Jane and Fred Vallier of Vallier Communications for another excellent job of editing.

To John Maghuyop, thank you for another great formatting and cover design.

Finally, to my readers, I sincerely believe in my quote, "When you stop dreaming or using your imagination, you start to die." I hope the adventures of Special Agent Jeannie Loomis and her team will inspire you to dream and use your imagination.

Enjoy!

"The larger crimes are apt to be the simpler, for the bigger the crime, the more obvious, as a rule, is the motive."

— Sir Arthur Conan Doyle

Prologue

On the night and following morning of July 16th–17th, 1918, in the Ipatiev House, known as the House of Special Purpose in Yekaterinburg, Russia, the Russian Imperial Romanov family consisting of Czar Nicholas II, his wife Empress Alexandra and their five children, Olga, Tatiana, Maria, Anastasia and their son Alexei, and all those who chose to accompany them into imprisonment, were shot and bayoneted to death.

The scene shocked the assassins, not because of the shootings, clubbing and bayoneting, but because the bullets they fired bounced off their targets. Unbeknownst to them, the Empress had sown the Romanoff jewelry into the fabric of their undergarments, causing the bullets to ricochet. Once the killing was over, the assassins were ordered to strip the bodies and turn the Romanoff gems over to Cheka, the secret police. The collection at that time was estimated to be over $500 million.

The Cheka discovered during an inventory in 1922 that three of the most expensive jewelry items had been stolen from the state vault: a sapphire tiara, a sapphire bracelet, and an emerald necklace. Suspicion fell on a Cheka officer who, while being detained and interrogated about the theft and whereabouts of the jewels, committed suicide. Following that, the trail of missing items went cold.

Chapter One

Awoman approached the podium and tapped on the microphone, drawing the attention of everyone in the larger of two briefing room. Those still standing made their way to chairs.

"Good morning. My name is Gloria Jamerson and I'm the director of Russian intelligence for the NSA. Let me begin by thanking you all for fighting the Washington D.C. traffic so you could attend this briefing."

Jamerson seemed to fit the stereotype of a long-time Washington bureaucrat and Clinton and Obama supporter. She wore what Pinheiro felt was an overly casual attire for a professional, especially one standing at a podium--a pair of worn slacks and a non-flattering blouse, and her hair needed a bleach job and styling. Former President Clinton started this craze when he took office, sometimes appearing in public dressed in less than business casual; but Obama took it to a whole new level, rarely wearing a suit and tie--his wife dressed like a thrift store model.

Looking over her shoulder to make sure all of the other speakers were in their seats, she returned to the microphone. "The individuals behind me will introduce themselves when they're up here. They represent agencies of the FBI, Interpol, NSA, DHS, CIA, and the Russian government."

Richard Pinheiro, an assistant director of the Department of Homeland Security, recognized many of the people behind Jamerson, but not a person who appeared uncomfortable and was surrounded by individuals providing national security for the United States. *At least he's dressed in a suit and carries himself professionally*, Pinheiro thought.

A large screen began descending from the ceiling to the right of the podium. Using a presenter, Jamerson pointed at a Mac computer resting on the podium. The screen showed a picture of an elderly man whom most in the room instantly recognized as Anatoly Pavlenko. "*Asshole*," Pinheiro thought to himself.

"If you don't recognize this man, his name is Anatoly Pavlenko. He was born in St. Petersburg, Russia, holds dual citizenship here in the U.S. and lives in this mansion in San Francisco (slide showing residence). The mansion was huge and Pinheiro knew it was located in the Pacific Heights area of the city, one of the most expensive areas in the United States.

The reference to San Francisco piqued Pinheiro's interest. The DHS, NSA, SFPD, FBI, and surrounding bay area law enforcement agencies had recently concluded their investigation into three jihadist teams' terrorist acts. Although one team had killed numerous Christians who flocked to the Russian Orthodox Church in San Francisco, the other two teams were terminated before they could act. This was when he met FBI agent Jeannie Loomis--now his girlfriend. He returned his attention to what Agent Jamerson was presenting.

"Our agency as well as the DHS, FBI, CIA and Interpol believe, but cannot verify, that he funds most if not all left-wing anarchists including Antifa, using income from his holdings in the Ukraine, former Soviet Union satellite countries, and Russia. He's into oil, gas, minerals--and for the purpose of this briefing--stolen property."

With that she turned and nodded to one of the gentlemen seated behind her who rose and moved toward the podium. He was wearing a black suit and red tie. Pinheiro thought that if someone looked up "Russian agent," they would see a picture of him. He had to be an FSB agent surviving the changeover from the former secret police--the KGB.

"Good morning," he said, "or should I say, Dobroye Utra?" Receiving few laughs, he introduced himself. "My name is Vasili Sokalov. I am with the Russian State Department."

Sure, you are, Pinheiro thought.

Sokalov advanced to the next slide showing a picture of a male, and obviously a royal. "For those of you who never studied Russian history, this picture shows our last Czar of Russia, Nicholas II. He was our last czar because Lenin"—advancing the slide—"and the Red Army forced his abdication from the throne during our civil war in March 1917."—advancing to the next slide--"This is the former royal family of Czar Nicolas." Using the presenter and laser beam, he circled each of the individuals in the photo. "This is the Tsarina Alexandra, and these are their four daughters, Olga, Tatiana, Maria, and Anastasia, and this was to be the heir to the throne upon Czar Nicolas's death, the Tsarevich Alexei who was a hemophiliac."—advancing to yet another slide--"This is the Ipatiev House, or to say it correctly, it was the Ipatiev House since it no longer exists. It was called the House of Special Purpose and I will tell you why it was named that in case you do not already know. It was a merchant's house located in Yekaterinburg, later renamed Sverdlovsk, about 1,784 km from Moscow. This is where the former Emperor Nicholas II of Russia, his entire family, and members of his household were executed in July 1918 following the Bolshevik Revolution.

"At one o'clock in the morning on July 17, 1918, the Romanovs were awakened by their personal physician, Dr. Eugene Botkin, who told them to quickly dress and gather their belongings to avoid the advancing White Army. The White armies that supported the tsar were on the outside of the town's border, and the booms of the big guns could already be heard.

"Once dressed, they were escorted by this man,-- advancing the slide-- Yakov Yurovskhy,

leader of the secret police, the Cheka, who had been sent to guard the family in the Ipatiev House. They gathered in the cellar, standing together almost as if they were posing for a family portrait. Alexandra, who was sick, asked for a chair, and Nicholas asked for another one for his only son, 13-year-old Alexei. Two were brought down to the room. Suddenly, 11 or 12 heavily armed men filed ominously into the room. Yurovsky pulled a piece of paper from his pocket with the order given to him by the Ural Executive Committee and read it aloud. It said, Nikolai Alexandrovich, in view of the fact that your relatives are continuing their attack on Soviet Russia, the Ural Executive Committee has decided to execute you.

"According to a guard's reminiscence, the Empress and Grand Duchess Olga tried to bless themselves, but failed amid the shooting. Yurovsky reportedly raised his Colt gun at Nicholas's torso and fired. Nicholas fell dead, pierced with at least three bullets to his upper chest. Another member of the killing squad shot and killed Alexandra with a bullet wound to the head, then shot Maria as she ran for the double doors, hitting her in the thigh. The remaining executioners shot chaotically and over each other's shoulders until the room was so filled with smoke, dust and noise that no one could see anything in the darkness nor hear commands. Within minutes, Yurovsky was forced to stop the shooting because of the caustic smoke of burned gunpowder and dust from the plaster ceiling caused by the reverberation of bullets and deafening gunshots. When they stopped, the doors were opened to scatter the smoke. While waiting for the smoke to abate, the killers could hear moans and whimpers inside the room. As it cleared, it became evident that the czar, the czarina and several non-family members had been killed. All of the Imperial children were still alive with only Maria injured."

Sokalov stopped talking and pulled a water bottle from under the podium and drank. He replaced the bottle under the podium and continued. "The noise of the guns had been heard by households all around, awakening many people. The executioners were ordered to use their bayonets, a technique which proved ineffective and meant that the children had to be dispatched with still more gunshots, this time aimed more precisely at their heads. The Tsarevich was the first of the children to be executed. Yurovsky watched in disbelief as one of the killers spent an entire magazine from his Browning gun on Alexei who was still seated transfixed in his chair. He also had jewels sewn into his undergarments and forage cap. The killer continued to shoot and stabbed him, and when that failed, Yurovsky shoved him aside and killed the boy with a gunshot to the head. The last to die were Tatiana, Anastasia, and Maria, who were carrying a few pounds (over 1.3 kilograms) of diamonds sewn into their clothing, giving them a degree of protection from the firing. However, they were speared with bayonets as well. Olga sustained a gunshot wound to the head. Maria and Anastasia were said to have crouched against a wall covering their heads in terror until they were shot. Yurovsky killed Tatiana who died from a single shot to the back of her head. Alexei received two bullets to the head, right behind the ear. While the bodies were being placed on stretchers, one of the girls cried out and covered her face with her arm. One of the killers grabbed a rifle and bayoneted her in the chest, but when it failed to penetrate he pulled out his revolver and shot her in the head. I am sorry if I am taking too long," he said while turning and looking at Jamerson who told him to take as much time as he needed.

"In the aftermath, it was clear to Yurovsky and members of the assassination team that the children's undergarments had jewelry sown into them, thus reflecting the bullets. He gave the order to collect all loose items from the blood and body waste on the floor and to bring them to his room, and ordered some members of the killing squad to strip the bodies of their clothing where even more jewelry was discovered.

Advancing the slide again, he continued, "This is the room where the assassinations took place.

"In the aftermath of the 1917 revolution, numerous reports in foreign newspapers suggested wanton vandalism and the loss of a collection reportedly worth five-hundred million dollars. Now, over a century after the Romanovs were assassinated by the Bolsheviks, the whereabouts of their jewelry remains a mystery. Which pieces made it out of the Revolution and into Europe intact? Which were pulled apart by the government and sold as stones? Which of the ones sewn into their clothing blunted the Bolsheviks bullets? Where are they all now? This remains a developing story. Catalogues created in 1922 and now the property of the USGS library in Virginia, contain images of three pieces including a sapphire tiara, a sapphire bracelet, and an emerald necklace that were missing from the 1925 inventory conducted in Moscow. Here is a picture of the missing items." Sokalov advanced the slides one-by-one to show the three missing pieces of jewelry.

Taking another sip of water, he looked at the crowd before him and continued, "In 1925, upon discovering the theft of these items, our investigators focused on this man—advancing the slide--Alexander Orlov who worked in the room that contained the safe and where the jewelry was housed. Unfortunately, during the interrogation period he was found hanged in his cell."

Yeah right, Pinheiro thought. *You mean during his torture he decided suicide was his only escape.*

"Our government has conducted an ongoing attempt to locate the missing jewelry. Recently, we received information that in 1925 the jewelry was in the possession of a relative of Anatoly Pavlenko who lived in St. Petersburg. By the time we got this information, however, he had died of old age, and neither his wife nor former mistress could provide additional information. In searching his house, we found a note hidden in a book referring to the transfer of Romanoff items to Yakov Yurovskhy for a much smaller sum of money than the jewelry was valued. We believe the missing jewelry items were then stolen by Alexander Orlov and sold to the father of Anatoly Pavlenko who currently has the Romanoff jewels." With that, he turned to Jamerson and walked back to his seat.

"Thank you, Mr. Sokalov, for your comprehensive review of the stolen gems. The Russian Government has asked for our help in locating and retrieving those items and learning more about Pavlenko's involvement. We have packets for each of you to take back to your agencies, hoping you can use whatever resources you have to further this investigation. As usual, the NSA and other intelligence agencies are available to assist." She looked at staff members located on the west wall and nodded to them. They quickly picked up packets and began distributing them.

Chapter Two

The flight from San Francisco to Miami International airport was long and exhausting due to a layover in Atlanta. Ismail and Jeannie hailed a cab to the Biltmore Hotel in Coral Gables where two rooms had been reserved. Ismail had already taken some good humor flack when he boarded the plane in San Francisco for wearing a Kansas City Chiefs jersey. Most of the passengers on their flight were bound for Super Bowl LIV to support their San Francisco 49ers. Jeannie was one of them.

Homeland Security agent Richard Pinheiro had surprised Jeannie with tickets for the big game once the two teams were announced. It was going to be their first official romantic get-away following the three terrorist acts in the bay area. Fortunately, only one bombing was successful in San Francisco where a crowd of the faithful were killed outside a Russian

Orthodox church hosting the pontiff. A second planned attack at the Cow Palace where the U.S. president was holding a fundraiser was prevented by Jeannie and her team and a very observant sniper. To prevent panic, the third attempted attack was never publicly reported. The terrorists were in the process of blowing up the BART underwater tube connecting San Francisco to Oakland.

"I can't believe I'm here," Ismail said. "Look at all the fans."

"Yeah, most of them are Niner fans if you've noticed," Jeannie replied.

"Nah, you need to get your eyes checked boss. Those are Chief jerseys, not 49ers," he said. "Can you believe my cousin, your boyfriend, got these great tickets for us?"

"Just remember buddy. Ricky got these tickets for him and me. He got called away on a case and I invited you. You're welcome," Jeannie said.

"Boy, does that mean I'm indebted to you for the rest of my life?" Ismail asked.

"Absolutely," she replied with a smile.

Tailgaters were operating full-force in the parking lot outside Hard Rock Stadium. One guy was deep-frying a whole turkey. Another had ribs, chicken, and corn-on-the-cob on his grill, and the aroma was out of this world. Tailgaters seemed to be competing with each other, but all in good fun.

"Gee, I don't see any Portuguese food," Ismail said, but before Jeannie could respond, one of the cooks yelled that he had some.

Ismail turned to see a Kansas City Chiefs fan plating up breakfast for him containing scrambled eggs, hash browns, and a link of linguica. "Hey, a fan with good taste both in his team and his food," Ismail said after thanking the cook. "See, you're rooting for the wrong team," he said to Jeannie while taking his first bite. She just rolled her eyes.

Another cook wearing a Joe Montana jersey near his motorhome overheard the banter, and not to be outdone handed Jeannie a pulled-pork sandwich and soda. She thanked him and accepted the sandwich and diet Coke since she did not want to offend him. Once in her hand, the sandwich smelled so good she was glad she accepted.

"Thank you, cousin," Ismail said while taking another bite.

Judge Swartz left his downtown office, looking forward to getting home in time for the big game. He did not care which team won. If the Chiefs came out on top, it would be their first Super Bowl win, and if the San Francisco 49ers pulled it off, their dynasty was on the rise again. He had chicken wings marinating at home with chips, beer, and nacho cheese as compliments. At halftime he would switch over to homemade submarine sandwiches and his famous chili. Walking to his Audi A6, he noticed the overhead light above his parked vehicle was out. *I'll have to tell maintenance about that on Monday*, he thought to himself. The underground garage smelled of exhaust fumes, motor oil, and rubber. Reaching his car, he placed his briefcase down next to the passenger front door while reaching into his pocket for the electronic car-lock fob.

From the darkness a figure emerged dressed in black from head to toe. The black ski mask only had cutouts for his eyes and mouth. A plastic bag containing a Ruger .22 caliber semi-automatic with suppressor was held in the figure's right hand. The bag would catch the expended shell casings. Walking slowly behind the judge, he fired a round into the back of the judge's skull. The judge was dead before hitting the cold parking lot floor. The figure walked up to the still body and pointed the weapon at the judge's heart, and fired one additional round and left the garage, carefully avoiding all overhead cameras. *The Star Chamber court will have one less judge as of today*, Joey thought. He removed his gloves but kept the ski mask on for a few minutes after exiting the parking garage in case there were other cameras activated.

At halftime the two teams were tied 10-10. "Looks like it's going to come down to the wire," Jeannie said as she got up to make a phone call to Pinheiro, use the restroom, and pick up something to eat.

"Yeah, but the Chiefs will turn it on in the second half. You watch," Ismail said.

The person behind him wearing a Niner's jersey, said, "Only if the referees continue to blow calls."

"Hi, how are the seats?" Pinhiero asked immediately after answering the phone.

"They're great, but a guy sitting next to me is a pain in the ass," she said, trying to suppress a laugh.

Pinheiro laughed. "Is my cousin getting under your skin?" he asked.

"Yeah, because I'd rather have you sitting next to me," she responded. "How was your briefing?"

"It wasn't bad. Do you know much about Russian history?" he asked.

"I took a course in it when I was an undergraduate. Why?"

"Well the briefing was about the theft of the Romanoff jewelry. You know, the last Czar of Russia and the assassination of his entire family," he said.

"Yes, it was fascinating learning about their civil war and what happened to Czar Nicholas II and his family. Did they talk about Rasputin?" Jeannie asked. "That guy had a lot to do with destroying the royal monarchy."

"No, I don't remember them talking about Rasputin, but the presenter went into a lot of detail about the assassinations, including how the assassins' bullets couldn't penetrate the Czar's daughters' undergarments," Pinheiro replied.

"Yeah, what a tragic time. After the assassins killed the royal family and a few of their servants, if I remember correctly, they loaded the victims into trucks and threw them down some mine shafts or well. They poured acid on the bodies, but were upset with the results so pulled them up and burned them. Why were you given a short history of the Russian Revolution?" Jeannie asked.

"There are three pieces of Romanoff jewelry stolen in 1925 that are worth millions, and the Russian government, aka the FSB, are fingering Anatoly Pavlenko as the one who has them," Pinheiro said.

"That asshole!" Jeannie said. "Yeah, I can see him being involved with stolen Romanoff jewelry. We both know he's into anything and everything to fund Antifa and any other radical left-wing group. He's probably using the gems as collateral or something. Shit, his house in Pacific Heights is on the market for $34 million dollars. His wealth came from his father who some believe played both sides of the Nazis and Russians during World War II. I'd love to see him take the fall. Hell, he's in his late eighties or early nineties, so a prison term would equal the death penalty. So, the briefing was to track down the missing gems and tie it to him, huh?"

"Something like that," Pinheiro said. "I'm not sure how the DHS fits in, except possibly having a chance to connect him with Antifa or the other groups he funds, maybe to get him on a RICA violation or conspiracy. I'm taking the packet they gave me back to the department and run it up the flag pole. We'll see what the higher-ups want to do with it. You two flying back tonight or tomorrow?" he asked.

"We changed our flight from the one you got us to an upgraded direct flight to San Francisco. We'll leave early tomorrow morning, but with the expected jet lag I won't go into the office until the next day. God, I miss you," Jeannie said.

"I miss you a whole bunch too, Pinheiro said. "Better get back to the game and tell that person sitting next to you that if he messes with you, I'll kick his ass."

"Will do," Jeannie said while blowing a kiss into the phone. "Love you."

"Love you too," Pinheiro said as they ended their calls.

Chapter Three

Primary threats to the United States are lone wolf jihadists. They are the hardest to track and they hide in the shadows--in cyberspace and on extremist websites--where al Qaeda and ISIS try to recruit them. To hunt them down, the NSA and the FBI have to be online since this is where most of the radicalization of future jihadists occurs.

On February 4, 2020 at an undisclosed location, FBI counter-intelligence analyst Peggy Jacobs notified her JTTF (Joint Terrorism Task Force) supervisor Ruth Billingham to look at her computer screen.

"I found this unanimous post from a user calling himself Zaid Abu Sayyaf. What caught my eye are his last two postings. One, he's already in the United States, and two, he wants to attack the United States and serve as a soldier of al Qaeda as soon as possible."

Jacob's supervisor asked her if she had been able to pull up the source. "Yes," Jacobs said, "It looks like he's in Waco, Texas. He's signaling to other individuals to see if they can help him secure the tools, meaning guns and explosives, he needs for a planned attack. He yearns for action."

"Great! Waco again. Hope it doesn't turn into another Branch Davidian shootout," Billingham said, reaching for a phone on Jacob's desk and looking at Jacob. "Get me our Dallas field office. It's going to be critical for them to find out who he is and get his exact location. They can do a more in-depth analysis to see if he's a real threat."

Acting on information he received from Billingham, Agent Paul Wilson tracked the IP address to a 21-year old Jordanian named Omar Hassan on February 5th at the FBI field office in Dallas. He pulled up a passport photo of the suspected radicalized individual and began a more intensive background check. He placed the photograph of Hassan in the upper center of a white-board in the Dallas office briefing room and printed Hassan's full name under the photo with an aka of Zaid Abu Sayyaf. He then drew a line to the right and taped a photo of Hassan's father. Below Hassan was a Google overhead photo showing their three-bedroom, non-descript residence in a fairly isolated Waco outskirt area.

By eleven o'clock that morning, six additional agents had arrived in the briefing room. Last to arrive was Dani Shapiro, the SAC at the Dallas field office who had been there for over a year and had won the support of her staff as a hard, but fair supervisor. She did not offer praise unless someone did something outstanding beyond their normal duties; subsequently, her praise was taken seriously.

"What do we have?" she asked as she took a seat.

Wilson turned to the group after placing additional documents on the white-board. "OK." Agent Wilson started, "The JTTF found postings on one of the jihadists websites by this man--pointing to the white board--using the username Zaid Abu Sayyaf. As you can see, his real name is Omar Hassan, a twenty-one year old Jordanian who came to the United States about two years ago with his father." Pointing to Hassan's father, Wilson continued. "Hassan's postings are becoming more and more threatening, and he's trying to link up with someone who can provide him with bomb-making material and information about becoming an al Qaeda soldier. JTTF stated that his postings appear to be real, not just idle boasts. He idolizes the dead Osama bin Laden and wants help pulling off attacks, meaning more than one! The IP address attached to his postings suggest they're coming from this residence outside of Waco. After reviewing the postings forwarded to us from JTTF, it appears he may be the real deal."

"Thanks Paul. Nice job on the workup. OK, we need to put eyes on Hassan and track his every movement," Shapiro said. "Paul will come up with how much manpower you and the rest of your team will need to track him and to set up a tactical surveillance of his residence. Jesus, he lives in no-mans-land area and it will be hard to track him. Everyone out there probably knows everyone else. OK people, I'm making this a priority one investigation."

Agent James Robinson and four other agents began tracking Hassan. His normal travels took him from his home to a fast-food restaurant just inside the Waco city limits along the I35 corridor. On the third day of tracking, Robinson entered the restaurant to observe Hassan close up. He waited 15-minutes after Hassan entered before entering himself, finding Hassan working the cash register and taking customer orders.

"Can I take your order?" he said when it was Robinson's turn.

"Yes, I'd like a burger, order of fries and a diet Coke," came the reply.

"Will this be for here?" asked Hassan.

"Yes, please."

"Would you like medium or large fries?" Hassan asked.

"Regular would be fine," Robinson answered, waiting to hear how much to pay. He found a table that would allow him to observe and hear Hassan interact with customers while waiting for his food. He ate while watching Hassan for almost a half-hour. Hassan was only 5'7" and thin, sporting what appeared to be a three to four days growth of facial hair. He appeared to be a gregarious outgoing young Arab man who could easily pass for a college student, but very unremarkable in any other respect. He did a good job of keeping the monster inside him well hidden.

The agents were correct. Trailing Hassan would not be easy. He lived in a rural area of Texas where there were few people on the road, forcing an increase in surveillance teams. When not at work, Hassan was online pleading for assistance with his jihad quest. Fearing he might link up with another terrorist cell, whether it be al Qaeda or ISIS, SAC Shapiro ordered an undercover Arab agent to contact Hassan via the Web and talk with him to see if he was the real deal. It was important to understand him and his motivations.

The legal department at the Dallas field office informed agents that the field office did not yet have enough evidence to make a case against Hassan. His defense would be that he was only exercising his 1st Amendment rights since no one had actually seen him typing his postings.

Chapter Four

Jeannie returned to her seat with her hands and arms cradling hot dogs and two beers, Ismail said, "What no nachos?"

"You're lucky you're getting this, wearing that Chiefs jersey," Jeannie responded.

"Good girl," said a lady wearing a 49ers jersey sitting behind her.

The half-time show started, and although Ismail liked the costumes worn by the two star performers and hoped for a wardrobe malfunction, he told Jeannie that he hoped his wife had the younger Flores children leave the room. "Gee, they call this empowering woman?" Jeannie asked Ismail. Ismail agreed that pole dancing was something that should stay in a strip club, not at a half-time show.

By the end of the 3rd quarter, the Niners were ahead 20-10 over Ismail's Chiefs which encouraged Jeannie to continue harassing him. "Still one quarter left," he would reply. Sure enough, the Niners took their foot off the accelerator and allowed the Chiefs to win the game.

"Oh well, they had a great season," Jeannie said to the lady behind her.

"Yeah, it sure looked to me that the referees were for the Kansas Chiefs with all the blown calls," came the reply.

Looking at Ismail who could hardly contain his smile, Jeannie told him to not say a word if he wanted to fly home the next day since she had the flight tickets. Ismail just bowed his head in silence while bump fisting another Chief's fan sitting next to him.

A butler answered the doorbell by opening the massive front door of Anatoly Pavlenko's mansion and invited the SDL (Sons and Daughters of Liberty) sergeant-of-arms to enter. He kept mental note of the number of security personnel he observed both outside and inside the estate. Pavlenko bought the original single-story house three years earlier, had it leveled to the ground, and methodically found an architect who promised to thoughtfully design a residence that would maximize inspiration, promote ease of living, and connect the city with the bay. The five-story architectural marvel that resulted was beyond doubt the most technologically advanced residence in San Francisco, environmentally designed to enhance physical, mental, and emotional health.

With four-bedrooms, three-and-a-half baths, and located in Pacific Heights, the house combined sophisticated luxury with leading-edge health and wellness accoutrements. The garden level of the home led to a private oasis. Stunning views atop the roof deck spanned from the Golden Gate to Alcatraz. Its interior had a technology-enabled platform for sustainable living, with custom finishes for modern tastes. The home was a vision for what an elevated living environment can be, especially for someone as wealthy as Pavlenko.

As the SDL member was escorted through the residence, he paid as much attention to the interior layout details as he had with the exterior design. While approaching the house he noted the modern façade and secured entryway with gas-lit pathway to the front door. The driveway had a secured entryway for three cars, the gate operated by a Siedal biometric keypad. There were two terraces, one facing north and the other south. The roof deck had sweeping bay views and a fire-pit culminating in a privacy-scaped outdoor entertainment area equipped with a large spa and television set.

All of the bedrooms were located on the top floor, each having a private exterior roof terrace entrance. When the former SDL leader entered the study, Pavelenko was sitting behind a huge carved cherry wood desk admiring three gorgeous jewelry items. "Joseph, how good to see you," Pavelenko said without rising from his chair. "Sit, sit. Would you like something to drink? Coffee, soda, water?"

"No thank you. And what do you have here?" he asked.

"Ah, these are the most beautiful jewelry items from the Romanoff dynasty. Do you know much about Russian history?" Pavelenko asked.

"No, nothing really," came the reply.

"Sad that your American schools do not spend time teaching European history anymore. I do not think they teach American history either. Am I correct?" Not waiting for an answer, he continued looking at each item with a magnifying glass. "During the Russian Revolution the Bolsheviks decided that the former Czar, Czar Nicholas II, and his family had to be assassinated. After the deed was done, all of the former monarchs' jewelry was confiscated by the new regime."

"Must be worth a ton," the SDL leader said.

"I have received estimates between seven-hundred million to one-billion dollars, but who knows."

"How did you get them? I'm sure the Russians had no intention of selling such items."

Laughing, Pavelenko put down the magnifying glass and said, "No, I can assure you that the former Soviet Union, and now the Russian government would never sell such items. There are many other pieces, some even more valuable than these, but I was able to secure these. Ah, but you asked how I got them, didn't you? My father obtained them from a source inside Cheka. Have you heard this name, Cheka?

"No, as I said, I know nothing about Russian history."

"The Cheka was the secret police of the former Soviet Union in 1925. Their name has changed over the years from Cheka to KGB to now, the FSB, but that is not important. My father became friends with one of the Cheka agents and offered him money to steal these items. After my father died, they became mine."

"What happened to the Cheka agent that stole the items? I'm sure the secret police did an investigation."

Waving his hand as if it were a trivial matter, Pavlenko said, "He killed himself while being interrogated. The Cheka were blood-thirsty I can tell you. But, by the time their investigation focused on him, these items were on their way to Germany, and eventually they ended up here in the United States. Would you like to look at them more closely?"

Walking around the desk to look more closely, the SDL leader made note of the wall mounted safe's model. He easily recognized the V-Line Quick Vault Locking safe and was familiar with its features. Not only was it made of a durable metal that allowed for safe storage, it was also bulletproof and drill and torch resistant. There was one adjustable shelf that allowed the owner to quickly and easily organize items such as the Romanoff jewelry. Plus, the shelf was removable if not needed. He loved the design of the safe: the door was indented and flush with the wall so that it could easily be hidden behind a painting or other hanging object.

The safe locks had a mechanical locking system that included an additional backup key. The push-button system allowed a person to create a unique code for gaining access. However, should owners find themselves in a situation where they forgot the code or needed to allow someone else access, a backup key was available. The safe was designed to be pry-resistant. No one could dislodge the door or pull the safe apart using a crowbar or similar object. Additionally, the hinges were mounted on the inside, making it nearly impossible to tear the door off. It was a fantastically designed safe he thought, but he knew of a way to gain access when the time came.

"You like, dah?" Pavelenko asked pointing at the gems.

"Yes, very nice," came the SDL leader's response as he walked back to his side of the desk. "I'm here because I need more funding for the event in Berkeley next week."

"The event on the University of California campus?" Pavelenko asked. "The one where the conservative talk show host will be present?"

"Yes, Megan Thompson. She's a rising star in the conservative talk show world and could command a large audience, which we hope to stop. I want to organize a group of forty Antifa members to mix in with the crowd both outside and inside the auditorium.

I think that twenty dollars per hour should attract enough bodies for the job."

"I am familiar with Ms. Thompson. Too bad. For an attractive intelligent woman, she does not understand the need for globalism." He opened a drawer in his desk and removed a metal box, one much smaller than the one that must have contained the Romanoff jewelry. Upon opening it, he pulled out a large bundle of $20 bills and split the bundle in half. Without counting, he handed it to the former SDL leader, asking if the murder of Swartz was his handy work. Pavelenko did not get a reply, only a smile as the SDL leader left the study--again paying close attention to his surroundings.

Chapter
Five

Returning to his safe house in Oakland, 31 year old Joey Rogers sporting a shaved head and Fu Manchu mustache, entered the kitchen where he found some of his cohorts sitting at the kitchen table including Amy Perry--a 24-years-old college graduate, former part-time model, and Joey's girlfriend--and next to her Billy Armstrong, Joey's 31-years-old former cellmate, both having served time in Folsom State Prison for armed robbery. Billy had long almost black hair that reached the small of his back, now in a ponytail. Joey did not think of himself as a mere assassin. He preferred to be looked upon as a coordinator--a leader of specialists--who in reality was the most cold-blooded of them all.

"We'll get some food after I tell you our plans for Berkeley next week and what I saw at Pavelenko's mansion today," said Joey.

"The motherfucker actually let you in his pad?" asked Vicki Sanders, the most radical member of the group. She was what some called a professional student--never having a job, just living and breathing on university campuses, chat rooms, or book stores on Telegraph Avenue. Anti-American, pro-Socialist, and an anarchy lover, she was the group's sparkplug who constantly had to be controlled by Joey. The oldest member of the group at 47, she still dressed like a hippy from the 1960s, but now streaked her long brown hair with either blue, green, or yellow highlights, and sometimes all three. She never failed to have a bitch about the U.S. government and was no fan of the sitting President.

"What was it like inside?" came the next question before Joey could answer the first. It came from Sandi Hayes, Sanders' lesbian lover. Only 18-years-old, she probably joined the group to punish her wealthy parents. She was the baby of the group and took all of her leads from Sanders. Before answering their questions, Joey asked where Chico was?

Chico Hernandez, a slightly obese 42-year-old Mexican-American, finally arrived and completed the group. Also an ex-con, Hernandez did time for a string of armed car robberies in the Los Angeles area. He was able to get some of the charges dropped and copped to a plea bargain, giving him ten years in prison which in the end only amounted to three and a half years. "Hey, we didn't have anything to eat so

I went and picked up some stuff," he said, carrying several large bags and a cup carrier with In-and-Out Burger food and sodas. "Anyone hungry?" he asked, putting items on the table. "Hell yes," said Billy who helped himself to the closest bag of goodies.

Joey continued to fill them in about his visit with Pavelenko, and the safe and jewelry he had seen. He did not feel the need to show them the large amount of cash stuffed in his rear pocket; it was for the UC event's recruitment.

"We're encouraged by your enthusiasm," typed the undercover Arab FBI agent from the secured computer lab inside the Dallas Field Office to Hassan. The Dallas FBI team wanted to see how far Hassan was ready to go. They needed to assess him quickly before he enlisted with al Qaeda or ISIS. The last thing the FBI wanted was for Hassan to hook up with either of them. "We are convinced that you have the talent necessary to be a soldier of al Qaeda. We are the only organization that can provide you with the tools and guidance needed for your jihad.

Hassan's lack of an immediate response was nerve-racking, but it gave the Dallas team time to dig up everything they could on him. He was born in Aljoun, Jordan. Initially he was close to his father but that disintegrated when his father divorced his mother and took him to Texas, leaving Hassan's friends and relatives behind. Their relationship was tenuous at best, but went downhill quickly after his mother died in Jordan. Thereafter, there appears to have been an uptick in his visits to known jihadist websites.

While working her way through a stack of phone messages, Jeannie heard a knock at her open office door. Looking up, she saw SAC Lomax. "How was the Super Bowl?" he asked. After Jeannie responded, he asked if she had time for a cup of coffee. She followed him to the breakroom on their floor and they took seats across from each other.

"There's going to be another major shake-up in the bureau next week. The President will appoint a new Attorney General and then heads will roll. The liberals will bitch and complain but the President will be in his right to hire and fire whomever he wishes. It appears by all reliable sources that he'll win re-election in a landslide, so he's about to flex his wings, not showing a bit of concern over the scam impeachment crap." He handed Jeannie a folded note listing several agent names assigned to their bureau. "These individuals will be notified this Friday at the close of business. Keep this confidential."

Jeannie looked at the names, knowing all of them. She was never impressed with their work ethic, production, or professionalism. "This will reduce our manpower until we get replacements," Jeannie said.

"Yes, but I've been assured by Washington that replacements will be here by mid-week, so barring any major events, we should be OK," he responded. Lomax's cellphone vibrated in his suit pocket. He pulled it out and saw Jamerson and a D.C. phone number on his display. "Huh." Addressing Jennie he asked, "Do you know anyone in D.C. with the last name of Jamerson?"

"Doesn't ring a bell," she replied.

"Well, I'd better call back and see what this Jamerson wants," he said as he rose and headed to the hallway leading to his office. Jeannie filled her coffee cup and was preparing to leave the breakroom when Darcy walked in.

"Hi Jeannie. How was the big game?" she asked.

"It was awesome! I know I lost a lot of what was shown on television, but the energy of over 68,000 people in a stadium rooting for their respective teams was unbelievable. Of course, starting tonight I'll watch the game again since I recorded it to see what I missed."

"Maybe not," said Lomax, overhearing Jeannie and returning to the breakroom. "I called Jamerson back and I need to see you two in my office." He waved a piece of notepaper in his left hand. "Find Flores and get him here also." With that, he turned and walked back to his office.

Chapter
Six

Agent Wilson finished addressing the task force at the Dallas field office by saying it appeared that Hassan was in the "jihad cool stage." Hassan loved what he was seeing on television and the Internet. It showed American soldiers being killed by al Qaeda and ISIS, and he could not wait to become one of their foot soldiers. He had his father, a new home, and especially a new country. He rejected the non-violent tenants of his religion and adopted the violent path of al Qaeda. He was ripe for radicalization and he was ready to carry out a violent act.

Weeks later, Hassan responded to the undercover agents' postings. The agents' carefully worded emails had attracted him. Hassan found a person who could fulfill his dream of becoming an al Qaeda soldier, believing he had contacted an al Qaeda cell. The undercover agent made Hassan believe that he was a lieutenant in the terrorist organization and that he had worked closely with former Osama bin Laden.

"If you are with me, I want to meet you, learn from you. But if you are American intelligence, you can go to hell," Hassan posted. Fearing they might lose Hassan, more and more emails were sent to him. Hassan continued to communicate, thinking he was truly communicating with an al Qaeda sleeper cell. A bonding had taken place, and Hassan expressed interest in even more possible target sites and his devotion to al Qaeda.

Still lacking hard evidence to justify an arrest, the Dallas team needed ongoing communication with Hassan until he made a significant move. Time was of the essence since he talked about the need to get handguns and high capacity clips. The task force worried that Hassan might become frustrated and carry out a lone wolf attack on a church, cinema, mall or even his workplace.

There was also the possibility that Hassan was playing the FBI for fools. His emails contained more and more calls for jihad, but the FBI had to avoid suggesting acts of violence. Such actions had to formulate in Hassan's mind alone. He, as an individual had to fully layout his plans. His intentions could not be perceived by a court as having been manufactured by the FBI. To avoid this, several communications took place in which the agent tried to talk Hassan out of committing a violent act. Each time, Hassan became agitated and displayed anger with the undercover agent. He was vehement in his desire to carry out a jihad act. He wanted to kill or cut the throats of Americans. Because of his increasingly violent rhetoric, Agent Wilson decided it was time to meet Hassan face-to-face.

Hassan was sent an email informing him there was an al Qaeda sergeant in the United States who would arrive in Dallas to meet with him. This would require Hassan to drive one and a half hours from Waco. This requirement, Agent Wilson felt, would later show the court that Hassan had plenty of time to back away from his request for violence. Hassan did not back off. He became excited about the future meeting. The undercover agent who had been talking with Hassan for several weeks posed as the sergeant.

A Four Seasons Hotel in Dallas was selected for the meeting. The parking lot provided a space for agents to monitor the arrival and departure of Hassan, and many of the suites had adjacent rooms with pass-through doors that agents could use in case something went wrong. Two days before the meeting, agents placed cameras and audio bugs in the designated room. In the adjoining room they installed monitoring and recording equipment.

On the morning they were to meet, Hassan was seen leaving his home and stopping at a nearby gas station. He went in to pay for his gas and returned to his vehicle carrying something to eat and drink.

The ninety-five mile drive would be hot since his car's air conditioning system did not work. He stopped twice on the way to Dallas. The surveillance team surmised that the time he spent inside the two fast-food restaurants was probably for bathroom breaks and to stretch his legs.

About two hours later, Agent Wilson and the task force heard surveillance team-one announce that Hassan had just driven into the hotel parking lot. Even with stops, he had made good time. He parked his car and walked quickly to the hotel entrance. "He's all yours, surveillance team-one out," came the alert.

Wilson acknowledged the transmission and told the team to get ready. "It's showtime," he said.

An agent in the hotel lobby said that Hassan had just entered the elevator and was heading up to the room. The monitoring and recording equipment was readied while the undercover agent waited for the knock on the suite's door. It came a short time later. Greetings in Arabic were shared, and the undercover agent motioned to the table where he had been sitting. No weapon was visible. It was now a make or break moment with thousands of American lives at stake. The ticking time-bomb who thought he was meeting with an al Qaeda sergeant was being recorded on equipment only a few feet away.

Hassan was very confident and showed no fear. He displayed no nervousness, only a coldness and eagerness to listen to the al Qaeda representative.

Their conversation was conducted in Arabic, so Wilson and the other task force team members were forced to peer over another Arabi FBI agent's shoulder who was translating and simultaneously typing the conversation into English. This, combined with the agent's body language was the only way for Wilson to interpret what was transpiring. Looks and glances were shared between the translator and Wilson. After only a few minutes the translator looked at Wilson and motioned that thy had a true believer and jihadist in the next room.

Hassan told the undercover agent that he had visited several buildings in Dallas and wanted to bring down a building like bin Laden did in New York. To do so however, he needed a large bomb, but he did not have the resources or material to get one alone. The undercover agent said he would relay Hassan's wishes to the new al Qaeda leader, and set up a second meeting the following week when Hassan was not working.

Hassan left satisfied that he had connected with an al Qaeda sleeper cell that would fulfill his dream of becoming not only a soldier of the infamous terrorist group, but also a person who would bring an American building to the ground, taking American lives in the process.

The lobby agent clicked his mic, alerting the mobile surveillance team that Hassan was about to leave the hotel. Agent Wilson opened the pass-through door between the rooms and asked the standing undercover agent, "What do you think?"

"Paul, I just looked into the eyes of Satin. This guy's going all the way. He's the real deal," came the answer.

The next day, online communication resumed. Wilson also briefed SAC Shapiro about the meeting. "We need to keep a tight net around this asshole," she said.

"Use all the resources you need. What about legal? Do we have enough to pick him up?"

"Not yet, "Wilson said. "They feel we still need more for an arrest, but they did give me the go-ahead to secure a search warrant."

"Won't that tip him off?" asked Shapiro.

"Not if you concur with how I would like to do it," he said. "My thought is that we hit the house when both Hassan and his father are absent. We don't do or take anything except copy Hassan's computer hard drive. We leave no trace of having been there. If we glean anything that can be used to get an arrest warrant, so be it--but if not, we can see what else he has on his computer."

"If legal signs off on it, go for it. Keep me in the loop," Shapiro said while returning to her office.

After the search warrant was obtained the following day, the surveillance teams followed both Hassan and his father as they left their residence. Once both Hassan was his father were at work, Wilson and two other agents hit the house. Fortunately, the father's bedroom window was left open. An agent climbed in and opened the front door.

The house was sparsely decorated with a used couch in the front room across from an off-brand flat-screen television, and smelled of Arabic spices. The single bathroom needed a deep cleaning. The agents found nothing of evidentiary value in the house until they entered Hassan's room. The room had been set up as a shrine to the dead al Qaeda leader Osama bin Laden. Pictures of now dead terrorists decorated every wall in the room. One showed bin Laden dressed in white, firing an AK-47.

The search warrant allowed for the uploading of Hassan's computer contents onto a thumb drive to be analyzed later. After 45-minutes, the search was concluded, and the agents left without a trace of their presence.

Panic overtook the task force team the following two days. Several emails had been sent to Hassan, but he had not replied. Wilson checked in with the surveillance team who earlier that morning had tracked Hassan to his workplace. "Is his car still there?" asked Wilson.

"Affirmed," came the response.

"OK, do me a favor. One of you two needs to go into the hamburger joint and put eyes on him. Order a burger and so on."

"Roger that. We're getting hungry anyway."

Wilson glanced at his watch and noted that it was 1:35 in the afternoon. Hassan normally works until 3:30. "Team leader--we have a problem."

Chapter Seven

Seeing Jeannie and Darcy already sitting in the room, Ismail entered Lomax's office without knocking. "Flores, I'm glad you're here," Lomas said. "I just started filling these two--motioning to Jeannie and Darcy—in about my phone call with Agent Jamerson of the NSA." There were no other chairs in Lomax's office, so Ismail stood next to the seated Darcy. "Our Dallas field office had been tracking a lone wolf terrorist named Omar Hassan. Darcy can give you the particulars later. They've concluded that he has been radicalized and on the verge of committing a terrorist act using a bomb."

"So, how do we fit in?" asked Ismail.

"They lost him," Jeannie said.

"What?" exclaimed Ismail.

"After months of tailing this guy with the tightest twenty-four seven net they could use in such a small town, he gave the surveillance team the slip from where he works," Lomax said. "They checked with his father and co-workers, but no one knows where he might be. The thought is that either Hassan or someone he works with spotted the surveillance teams and he spooked. For the past month he hasn't been on the Internet until last night. His IP address popped up here in San Francisco, and he's once again talking to one of our undercover agents. He said that he thought American intelligence was monitoring him, so he got out quickly. He's spent the last few weeks scouting new sites in our city for jihad, and wants the person he believed was part of an al Qaeda cell he met in Dallas to meet with him here, so he can carry out his plan." Lomax stopped talking and looked at the three agents before him.

"Jeannie, have you spoken recently with Pinheiro?" Lomax asked.

"No sir. I tried calling him a few times in the last several hours, but it always goes to voice mail," came her response.

Lomax continued, "It's probably because he's on a plane as I speak. Jamerson alerted the DHS, and Pinheiro's flying out here with the undercover agent from Dallas that previously met with Hassan." Jeannie felt excited about seeing Ricky and the time they would be able to spend with each other. She also felt she was blushing since she had plans for her Rickey when he arrived—an unexpected surprise to say the least.

"Darcy, I need you to connect with Jamerson or whomever she feels you need to work with from the NSA. We need to track down the location of his IP address. She said it was around San Francisco--but shit, that could mean South San Fran, Burlingame, Marin, Daly City, or Pacifica, just to name a few. Get Burk and have him gather all the intel the NSA and our Dallas field office has asap. I want everything they have on their walls posted in our briefing room. Have him get everything in place before Pinheiro and the Dallas agent gets here. Jeannie, you arrange for the pickup at the airport. I'm not sure of the flight number, arrival time or details. Ismail, once Darcy locates the IP address, do a quick drive by and see what type of place this guy's living in. Wait a minute..." Lomas said before starting up again. "...this guy might have spotted a bureau car used in his surveillance and is already spooked. Maybe Jeannie will loan you her Corvette for the cruise-by."

"Sounds great to me," Ismail said as he placed his opened hand in front of Jeannie with a big smile on his face. "Maybe I should change into my Kansas City Chiefs jersey to complete the charade." Jeannie rolled her eyes and fished the car keys out of her front pocket.

"OK. Get to work people," said Lomax as Jeannie and Darcy stood and followed Ismail out of the office.

Joey set up shop at a local Starbucks near the main UC campus. He scheduled 15-minute meetings with responders to his on-campus post, offering a $20 per hour activists' job. *How long does it take to convince a bunch of idiots to act out for a media group when they're offered that amount of money and a promise of legal assistance if they get arrested,* he thought? Sometimes Joey even offered a bonus if they get arrested. It was not his money anyway. It was the fat fuck Russian living in the mansion with stolen jewelry. All but one person excitedly took the job offer. They were to meet outside a coffee shop on Telegraph Avenue at 6:30 p.m. on Tuesday for final instructions, before marching onto campus shouting and assaulting anyone they felt like hitting. He encouraged them to wear masks or scarfs to protect their identity, as well as bats and clubs. Political signs would be provided to them at the coffee shop.

He then returned to their hideout and found Amy waiting for him. "How did it go?" she asked.

"Good. I think we have a lot of violent dumbasses who will create havoc tomorrow night." He grabbed her waist and pulled her towards him. "Anyone else in the house?" he asked.

"Not that I know of," Amy replied. Joey slid his hands under her white t-shirt and found she was not wearing bra.

"Then, let's not lose the opportunity," Joey said as he led her to their bedroom.

That evening, everyone was present in the front room. Joey told the group about the event scheduled the following evening and then broached a new subject. "We need cash and I have two ideas on how we might score some." No one spoke, and a few leaned forward in interest. "First, I think Anatoly Pavlenko is ready to be taken down. We just need a little more intelligence regarding his security staff and their number, their arrival and departure times, routine, and so on. Chico, I want you, Billy, Sandi, and Vicki to stake out the place from a distance for the next week. Do it in shifts so we can determine when his guards show up, when they leave, and Pavlenko's schedule if the prick keeps one. Once I'm satisfied we can hit the house successfully, we'll make our assault."

"You said you had two ideas," Amy said.

Joey continued, "Yes. The second one will be a little more complicated but it will take some of the heat off of us while we continue to kill off Star Chamber judges. Remember, we're avenging our comrades-- three whom the Star Chamber decided to eliminate as they erased their tracks. Our comrades did not betray them--they betrayed us." He realized he was shouting and stopped, then returned to his second idea. "Everyone knows Howard Sadler, correct?" he asked. "Sure, he's that wealthy son-of-a-bitch that started up the telecommunication business in Silicon Valley, right?" said Vicki. "He's worth north of one billion dollars. He makes his money by having sweatshops around the world make parts for his products, and then he sells them here and abroad for a ton."

"How are we going to rob him?" asked Hernandez. Everyone turned towards Joey waiting for his answer.

"We're not going to rob him. We are going to kidnap his teenage daughter and hold her for ransom. While I was in Berkeley today recruiting anarchists for the Megan Thompson show, I thought of a way to make some money as well as drive the cops crazy. How many of you know anything about the kidnapping of Patty Hearst?"

Sandi, Armando, and Amy looked clueless, but Vicki quickly answered his question. "Yeah, Patty Hearst and the SLA--the Symbionese Liberation Army, right?" Joey nodded his head, indicating for her to go on. "In 1974, Patty Hearst was shacking with her boyfriend Steven Weed in an apartment just off the Berkeley campus. The SLA was a group of 4-6 individuals who shared an ideology and hatred for the rich, along with their ex-con leader named Cinque. They came up with a plan to snatch Patty from her apartment and hold her for ransom, but they didn't ask for money. They made Patty's rich parents deliver free food to different locations in the bay area. Eventually, they were able to brainwash Patty into joining their group." Vicki looked at Joey and could see by his facial expression that he was satisfied with her answer.

"So, what? Are we going to kidnap her and make her parents give away free stuff?" asked Chico.

"No. Fuck the free stuff crap. Let Bernie Sanders offer that free shit to society. No, instead we'll ask for the money," Joey said looking at the group.

Chapter
Eight

J eannie got up at 6 a.m., and before showering she gave her nude body a once-over. *Looks like the gym is paying off,* she thought. She saw a few crow's-feet that edged a widened eye. She had accepted the merciless encroachment of age and was keeping her youthful-looking face and body, and had yet to see an ounce of fat. In her view and hopefully that of Ricky, she still looked as vibrant and alive as when she graduated from the FBI Academy. While driving to the airport she listened to KSFO, the only conservative talk radio show emanating from San Francisco. The two talk show hosts were describing how outrageous the Antifa crowd acted against innocent bystanders waiting in line to see conservative Megan Thompson speak at the University of California, Berkeley campus the day before. Twenty-nine were seriously injured and one elderly woman died of a heart attack--presumably brought on by the violence she witnessed. Once Jeannie arrived at the bureau, she spent the rest of the morning and afternoon making sure everything was in place for Ricky and Amir. She also touched base with the SAC to keep him up to speed.

Jeannie picked up Rickey and the Dallas agent from the airport arrival area in the early evening. Pinheiro introduced Amir Ramzi to Jeannie while placing both his and Ramzi's luggage in the back of the bureau's car trunk. Pinheiro climbed into the front seat of the car, not giving Ramzi the opportunity. "Hello agent Loomis. How have you been?" Pinheiro asked as he winked at Jeannie with his right eye so Ramzi could not see it.

"Fine. It's been a little while," she said, returning his wink. "You two are staying at the Hyatt Regency in Union Square right?" she asked.

"Yes. One thing about the DHS, they rarely put us up in a two-star hotel," Pinheiro replied.

"Amir, I guess we in the FBI can't say that, huh?" Jeannie remarked.

"No. I can say I've spent many nights in crappy motels fighting cockroaches to see who's got most of the bed," he replied in perfect English with no hint of a dialect.

"God, your English is phenomenal," Jeannie said, looking back at Amir in the rearview mirror while Pinheiro slyly rubbed Jeannie's right thigh, sending chills up her back and causing her to skip a breath.

"Thank you," Amir said. "My parents brought me to the States when I was only two-years old. We spoke both English and Arabic in our home, so I'm lucky to speak without the typical Arab accent when speaking with native Americans."

The rest of the drive to the Hyatt was Jeannie's rehash of what Lomax told them about Hassan, and the work she and her team had already completed. "His IP address was tracked down to a rundown three-story apartment complex in the Haight.

"I'm not familiar with the Haight. What is it?" Amir asked from the backseat as Ricky became more brazen with his hand movements on Jeannie's thigh.

"It's the name of a city district. Its full name is Haight Ashbury, home of the Hippie Movement in the 1960s. During that time every drop out and run away in the country fled to the Haight for drugs, free sex or to just drop out. Even old Charlie Manson hung out there for a little while. Even though the rent is becoming almost astronomical, the area still attracts rejects," Jeannie said.

"And now jihadist," Amir replied.

"And now jihadist," Jeannie said in agreement and continued, "Here we are gentleman." She waved off a concierge approaching their car as Amir and Pinheiro exited.

"Amir, why don't you go in and get settled. I want to meet with Jeannie's SAC for a few minutes at the bureau. Go ahead and order room service and charge it to my room since everything's under my name. I'll catch up with you tomorrow morning for breakfast, say eight a.m.?

"That sounds good to me. See you both tomorrow morning," Amir replied. If he suspected anything more than two colleagues talking about work, he did not show it. Amir grabbed his bag and headed into the hotel.

"That was smooth," Jeannie said as Pinheiro re-entered the bureau car. Pinheiro looked at the hotel entrance, and not seeing Amir, leaned into Jeannie and gave her a long passionate kiss. "Did you really want to see my SAC? He's probably already left for home," Jeannie commented.

"No, what I want to see is the inside of your bedroom," Ricky said, giving her another kiss.

"So you think we can knock off Pavlenko's house?" Amy asked Joey. "It's huge, and Vicki said she and Sandi counted four security officers on duty each shift."

"Yes. With the information the four of them gathered this past week, I think I have a plan that I'll share with everyone tonight. Take this--handing her a $100 bill--and pick up three or four pizzas and drinks, and I'll fill everyone in at dinner."

Having completed their last shift of the Pavlenko house-watch, Vicki and Sandi with Chico's help approached Judge Wayne Katamoto's backyard.

Chico, the tallest of the three, peered over the fence and saw the Judge lying in a lounge chair asleep next to his koi pond and waterfall. Katamoto retired from the bench two years ago, but quenched his enduring thirst for justice through involvement with the Star Chamber. Meeting in secret, the court tried defendants in absentia who felt they were above the law due to their political or celebrity status. In recent months the court had to suspend their proceedings indefinitely due to circumstances involving the arrest of Judge Baldwin, a Star Chamber judge, for child pornography. With converging law enforcement, the court went dark.

Chico reached over the fence and released the locking mechanism, allowing Vicki and Sandi to follow him through the open gate. Sandi was amazed at the koi pond's crystal-clear water, the beautiful fish swimming near the surface and the soothing sound of the waterfall. Although for most people a bee sting is painful but relatively harmless, for individuals like Judge Katamoto, an insect sting can trigger a potentially deadly anaphylactic reaction--especially if it contains one-hundred times the usual amount of venom between 5 and 50 micrograms.

Vicki removed a syringe from a pouch she wore as a purse around her waist and shook it, noticing a small air bubble in the solution. *Shit!* she thought. *That'll be the least of his problems.* With Chico standing in front of Katamoto and Sandi behind the judge's head, Chico jumped and crashed down on the judge's stomach, knocking the air out of his lungs. Katamoto tried to move while in shock, but the weight of Chico held him down while Sandi held his head and kept his mouth shut, allowing Vicki to inject the poison into the side of his neck. Katamoto was no match for Chico, and within minutes Katamoto's body began to convulse with froth spewing from his mouth and nose through Sandi's fingers. His body soon went limp and the Star Chamber was down another judge.

Confirming that Katamoto was dead, the assassins admired the swimming koi and the numerous bonsai-styled trees surrounding the pool. "If you're going to die, what a peaceful place to do it," Vicki said as she placed the syringe in her pocket. They took a few more minutes to admire the backyard and then retraced their steps without a trace.

Chapter Nine

Their lovemaking went on for hours. First it was passionate, then it turned animalistic. Exhausted, Jeannie laid in Ricky's arms, playing with the hair on his chest. "God, I missed you. Here I was at the damned Super Bowl with your cousin, watching my 49ers blow their lead and eventually lose the game, and all I did was think of you."

"It's nice to be wanted," Ricky replied. "So, how bad was my cousin?"

Jeannie laughed, saying that since Ricky could not be there, Ismail was the logical replacement. "That guy can eat, I'm telling you. Three hotdogs, one helping of nachos, and three beers. Oh, I forgot. He also got a bought hot-fudge sundae."

"That's my boy. And you know, he never puts on weight," Ricky said, laughing.

"I asked him about that, and you know what the little perv said?" Jeannie asked, not expecting a response. "He said that when you have an Alpha-sex drive like him, the calories just naturally come off." Pinheiro laughed so hard, Jeannie had to get off his chest.

"He said that?" Ricky asked, still laughing.

"You find that funny, do you?" Jeannie said, pinching one of Ricky's nipples.

"Ouch!" Ricky yelled. "You know though--how many kids does my cuz have now?"

"Oh God, you're just as pathetic as he is. Both Portuguese perverts," Jeannie said as she slid her hand down over Ricky's groin and found him hard again. After another round of lovemaking, there was an uneasy quiet in the room, as if both were in deep thought.

Jeannie was the first to break the silence by asking Ricky what he was thinking. "A hot-fudge sundae," he said laughing.

"Do you want another pinch?" Jeannie asked, starting for his right nipple again.

"No, no! I was just kidding," Ricky took a deep breath and said, "Gee, I didn't know you were into masochism." Jeannie grabbed his groin again and said she could pinch there as well. "No, no. OK, I was thinking that I'm falling in love with you. There, I said it." Jeannie did not know what to say. "You're awfully quiet," Ricky said as he placed one hand around Jeannie's waist and the other on the top of her head. Jeannie was laying on her back. Ricky noticed a tear falling from her left eye. "Did I say something wrong?" he asked.

"No, it's not you. It's me," Jeannie said. "You know I'm a two-time loser when it comes to long-term relationships. I try to tell myself it's the job, the travel, the rush, or trying to catch the bad guys, but maybe it's just me. Maybe I just don't understand what love is." Quiet filled the room again. "Come on big guy. What does love mean to you?" she asked.

Taking a deep breath and sitting up in bed with his back to the headboard, Ricky said that the best definition he ever heard about love came from a man who called into a talk show hosted by a female psychologist whose name he forgot. "There were some fruitcakes that called in saying that love was wanting to jump the bones of your significant other all the time. Other males said true love was having a wife that never got headaches when they were horny. And then a man called in and had a hard time communicating what he had to say. His definition of love was being there when his wife discovered a lump in one of her breasts. Love was being with her when she visited her doctor who recommended a mammogram. Love was sitting next to his wife when the doctor recommended a biopsy, and love was waiting with his wife for the results which seemed to take days. Love was going to the doctor's office and learning with your wife that the biopsy came back positive—malignant, and that she needed to have an immediate mastectomy. Love is being at her side, waiting for the anesthesia to wear off. And love is

GARY J. ROSE

going with her to buy a specialty bra so the breast removed is not obvious.

"The caller became so choked up that the psychologist told him to take a few breaths before continuing. After a pause, he continued by saying that love is being there when your wife's doctor informs her the cancer has spread and she needs chemotherapy. Love is sitting by your wife's side holding a bowl below her chin as she vomits after chemo treatments, and love is laughing with your wife as more and more of her hair falls out. The laughing continues as you and your wife select a wig she hopes will not be needed when her hair grows back. Love is the joy you two share when the doctor tells you the cancer is in remission. The caller again choked up and regained his composure more quickly this time. Love is when the doctor calls requesting to see your wife in his office. Love is learning that the cancer has returned. Love is watching your wife's weight tumble as the prescribed treatments fail. Love is being told your wife needs hospice. And finally, love is holding your wife's hand and hearing her last words, I love you, before she joins the angels.

"That's the best definition of love I've ever heard, and that's how I see it as well," Ricky said as he turned to look at Jeannie, waiting for a comment.

Jeannie was not sure what to say as she teared up, her mascara running into her eyes, down her cheeks, and staining the top sheet she had used to cover her nakedness. Tearing led to sobbing and shaking. Ricky

64

pulled her into his arms and stroked her hair. She swung her right leg over his legs and said, "I love you so much," as they drifted off to sleep.

The next morning Jeannie woke to the aroma of something cooking in the kitchen downstairs. She grabbed her robe, pulled her hair back into a ponytail and headed downstairs to investigate. Ricky was in his sweatpants and t-shirt, scrambling eggs while strategically trying to keep the fried potatoes and linguica separate from each other. As he entered the kitchen, the toaster popped up four slices of toasted bread. Ricky had already called Amir at the hotel and told him to grab a cab and meet him at the bureau since he had gotten an early start.

"Good morning sunshine. I hope you're hungry," Ricky said with a big smile.

"I'm famished," Jeannie replied. "You didn't have to get up and make breakfast, but I love it."

"Wait until you taste it. You may hate it," he responded, plating the breakfast on two plates and taking them to the kitchen table. Before sitting, he poured two cups of coffee.

"God, this is so good!" Jeannie said. "Linguica even. Your cousin would be proud of you."

"Well, you know, us alpha male-sex machines need to keep our weight off while restoring our vital nutrients."

"You're a pervert, just like your cousin," Jeannie said, taking another mouthful. Right on cue, Jeannie's cellphone went off on the counter where she had placed it the night before. Normally it is on her nightstand next to her bed, but passion got in the way and her routine was disturbed. Grabbing the phone and quipping to Ricky, "Speak of the devil," she answered with, "Hey you. What's up?"

"I know my cousin stayed with you last night, so I think I'm supposed to ask, what's up," Ismail said, suppressing a laugh.

"God! Both of you need therapy," Jeannie said, smiling at Ricky. "What did you find out?"

"Well, little bin Laden lives in a crappy flat on the third floor in the Haight," Ismail reported. "His room faces the rear, but he can only come and go through the front door. The place isn't up to code since there's no fire escapes from either the second or third floor. His mailbox is blank, but I talked to a friendly soul who told me that Hassan recently moved it. Setting up surveillance shouldn't be too hard. There are a lot of homeless encampments on the street. You want to order surveillance now?"

"Hang on one-minute while I check with Ricky," she said. Ricky agreed and she told Ismail to stay in the Haight until the surveillance team showed up, and when they did, he was to get back to the office.

"Roger that boss. Oh, and ask my cuz if he slept well last night?" Jeannie just hung up.

After breakfast they took a shower together and that led to another tumble in the hay before showering solo and getting ready for the drive across the Dumbarton Bridge into the city. Jeannie showered first and started to blow her hair dry, but finally just put it in a ponytail to be done with it and on her way.

Pinheiro walked outside while Jeannie made sure everything was locked up. Ismail still had Jeannie's Vette, she left the bureau car in her driveway. Closed the front door, she saw Delores, her next-door neighbor and watchdog, quickly converging on Ricky. "Hi, Jeannie. How are you?" Delores asked as she looked Ricky up and down. "And who do we have here?" she asked. *Shit!* Jeannie thought. The neighborhood gossip will make sure everyone knows she had a sleepover. She would have made a great minuteman during the American Revolution when she could have alerted the Continental Army that the British were coming.

"Hi Delores, I'm fine. How are you?" Jeannie said, trying to avoid Delores' question about Ricky.

"Hi, I'm Ricky Pinheiro. I work with Jeannie from time to time," he said as he offered his hand to Delores. Delores began blushing, realizing her hair was still in oversized curlers.

"Oh, nice to meet you," Delores said. "I'm Jeannie's next-door neighbor--pointed to her house--I watch Jeannie's house and put out the garbage when she's tied up. Well, I don't mean tied up," she said, absentmindedly touching her curlers and then fanning her face. "Oh my, I think it's going to be hot today. Well, you guys have a nice day, and Jeannie don't forget to let me know if you need anything. I'll talk to you later." She turned and walked back to her house, stopping on two occasions to get a better look at Ricky.

"She seems nice," Ricky said as he got into the front passenger's seat.

"Ugh! You have no idea," said Jeannie as she got behind the wheel and began backing out of the driveway, seeing Delores push the Venetian blinds in her front bay window open just enough to get a better view.

With all six in the kitchen, Joey asked Chico, Vicki and Sandi how the operation went with Judge Kanamoto. "It was a breeze," Chico said. "The old fart never knew what hit him." Sandi and Vicki nodded in agreement.

"Good, two down and six to go," Joey remarked. He briefly left the room and returned with a three by four foot piece of white cardboard that he placed on the table which Amy and Billy had cleared. "Here's the exterior and interior of Pavlenkos' house. You say you hourly saw security personal walk outside, check the perimeter and sides of the house, and then return inside, correct?" Vicki, Sandi, Billy, and Chico all nodded yes.

"That means there are only two inside the house with Pavlenko. This pattern doesn't seem to vary, only that new personnel arrive in twelve-hour shifts. That's good. The alarm system's inside the house on the second floor and monitored by one of the two inside guards. Pavlenko's normally in his third-floor study. Here's how we're going to do it."

Chapter Ten

Pinheiro held Jeannie's right hand during the drive from Newark to San Francisco. Traffic was heavy and they were about thirty-five minutes late, but neither of them complained.

Pinheiro and Jeannie found Amir in the breakroom, and just as they were getting seated, Jeannie's phone when off. It was Ismail. "What's up Ace?" Jeannie asked.

"Hey, you're not going to believe this, but legal is asking you and me to meet with the scumbag judge. You know, Baldwin in federal lockup. He wants to make a deal and will give us some information about the Star Chamber and the Sons and Daughters of Liberty, the SDL, for an easier sentence on the child porn rap. They want to know if we can attend a meeting with them and Baldwin at 1300 hours today. I told them it shouldn't be a problem, but if so, I'd call them back."

"No problem. That should be OK," Jeannie said.

Disconnecting from Ismail, she told Pinheiro and Amir about the request. Pinheiro was familiar with the Star Chamber investigation and how the court disappeared along with the assassins known to be the enforcement branch of the organization. Apparently, the SDL also went into hiding. Both he and Jeannie filled Amir in about the former investigation, since his knowledge only came from the media. "I wonder what the prick will give up," Jeannie asked.

Finishing her coffee, Jeannie checked in with Tami, her receptionist, to get phone messages. With Pinheiro and Amir in tow, Jeannie checked to see if Lomax was in his office. He was not. Tami told them he was in the briefing room with Burk and Darcy. The three proceeded to the briefing room and saw Darcy and Burk pointing to items taped to the white-board. "Sorry for being a little late," Jeannie said. "The traffic was a bear this morning."

From what was displayed on the white-board, the three could see that Burk and Darcy had been busy. The two had pretty much duplicated the display wall at the Dallas field office, having Googled front and rear area overhead photos of the Haight apartment complex. Ismail arrived and grabbed a cup of coffee and took a seat. Lomax confirmed that Jeannie had ordered a 24/7 tactical surveillance team in place. He turned to Pinheiro and asked his opinion on how to proceed?

Jeannie got a closer look at the Hassan photograph. There was something about the density of his eyes that struck her--black holes where everything gets sucked in and nothing comes out, suggesting a hiding place for evil.

"First, I have to compliment your team for a great workup," Pinheiro said as he waved toward the whiteboard. "We need to quickly set up a computer for Amir so he can re-establish communication with Hassan. This will buy us time and allow your surveillance teams to record his movements here in the city."

Lomax looked at Jeannie who got the cue and said. "OK, Darcy, Burke. Why don't you take Amir and get him set up with whatever he needs. Ismail, take Ricky, I mean Pinheiro, in the Vette and show him the lay of the land. I'll alert the surveillance team that you two will be cruising the area." She turned her attention back to the Hassan's photo and said, "Let's just hope he hasn't already found a target and is ready to carry out his jihad."

It was the first time for Pinheiro to ride in Jeannie's hot Corvette. "So, you and boss lady got something going, huh?" Ismail asked. Before Pinheiro could answer, Ismail continued. "You know, she's not only a fantastic boss, but probably my best friend besides my wife."

"First, if you're concerned that I'll hurt her, you don't have to worry. I told her last night I've fallen in love with her," Pinheiro confessed to his cousin.

"Wow, that's great!" Ismail said. "I think you two would be good for each other. When's the big day?"

"Slow down cuz," Pinheiro said, smiling and looking out the window. "We've only been together a short time, but there's a lot of chemistry between us. We haven't even discussed how to handle a long-distance relationship. You know how much I have to travel for the job and being stationed in D.C. We've decided to take it slow. But God, I volunteer any chance I get to fly out. You know, they were going to send another agent instead of me, but I pulled rank just to be here with her."

"Sounds like you got it bad, brother," Ismail said as he ran through the gears of Jeannie's Vette. "We're getting close to Hassan's dumpy apartment. Hey, if we ever get some free time, I want you to bring Jeannie to our house for dinner. My wife would love that."

"Sounds good to me. Maybe your wife will make me some malasadas. What do you think?" Pinheiro asked as they neared their destination. Hassan's apartment was located on Oak Street. Ismail drove up and down the street three times so that Pinheiro could see the layout from all angles. "How the fuck could this prick afford an apartment here?" he asked. "I mean, what's the rent here anyway?"

"Bro, some of these places go for over eight-thousand per month. Can you believe it? And this isn't even close to the nicest places in the city. I suspect, but of course we won't know until we get into his apartment, that he's living in a large apartment closet without the landlord or owner knowing he's there."

"What do you mean, not know he's there?" Pinheiro asked.

"See, it's like this. I rent an apartment for say, thirty-five hundred a month. That's a lot of money for one person, so what I do is clear out my closet and rent that space for say fifteen hundred a month, helping me with the rent. The guy who rents it probably doesn't like it, but it beats commuting back and forth over the bridge to the east bay. In exchange for his rent, he has a place to sleep, bathroom and kitchen privileges, all without the landlord being aware. Knowing what I know about this fuck, he probably piggy-backs on the legal apartment renter's Internet and he's in business."

"Son-of-a-bitch! Fifteen-hundred a month, just to live in a closet. Unbelievable!" Pinheiro said as he took one last look at the complex. "How do you and Jeannie do it?" he asked.

"Hell, like all the other agents in the San Francisco bureau, we had to find a place across the bay. We can't afford to live here. But actually, I wouldn't want to live is this shitty city anyway. The fucking liberal city government has turned the city into a third-world country." Just then they saw a male pull down his pants near the curb and shit all over the sidewalk and street. "See what I mean?" Ismail said. "Do you know the SFPD doesn't even respond to car burglaries anymore? One of my friends on the force told me they get a car burglary call every twenty-two minutes."

"Damn," said Pinheiro. "That's worse than D.C. But you know, that brings up something I didn't think about. How is Hassan getting around? Does he have a car, a motorcycle, or is he using public transportation?"

"I'm sure our surveillance teams will let us know. Let's get back to the bureau, but since I have your girlfriend's car I think we need to take the long way back," Ismail said, gunning the Vette's engine.

"Agent Loomis, Flores. I'm glad you could make it on such short notice," said Peter Stevenson, one of the best legal minds in the city's federal prosecutor's office. "Let's go in here so we can talk before meeting with Baldwin and his attorney." Jeannie was glad Stevenson did not refer to Baldwin as a judge. He was a child rapist and pedophile and no longer deserved to be referred to as a magistrate in her mind.

"I got a call last night from his attorney, Andrew Kaufman, who said his client wished to make a plea deal. As I told Agent Flores, he's willing to give up information about the Star Chamber and, let's see--glancing at his notes--the Sons and Daughters of Liberty. I assume that would be of great interest to the FBI."

"Yes, it would," Jeannie said. "Our investigation came up short. When we hit this secret court's prior location they had already cleared out, leaving no leads. The only information we had came from our informant before he died. He was a member of the SDL."

"I see. Well, I don't want to be locked into a plea deal unless you two feel it's justified based on what he might provide. What about doing this? I'll inform him and his counsel that he has to give up something tangible before we can even begin to discuss a deal. We'll take a break and reconvene, and you can tell me what you think. Is that OK with you?" Stevenson asked. Jeannie and Ismail affirmed.

Stevenson entered the slightly larger of two conference rooms followed by Jeannie and Ismail who were admitted by a uniformed officer. Baldwin sat with a smirk on his face. Next to him was Kaufman, a sharply dressed young male whom Jeannie thought to be in his mid-forties. He rose and shook hands with Stevenson who introduced Jeannie and Ismail. Everyone took a seat. Jeannie could feel Baldwin's eyes staring at her instead of his counsel or the federal prosecutor. *Still trying to intimidate, huh asshole!* she thought.

"Mr. Baldwin," Stevenson said. "It's Judge Baldwin, if you don't mind," said an obvious adversarial response from the former judge. Stevenson did not correct himself but instead continued. "Your attorney, Mr. Kaufman, has informed me that you wish to give up some information about the secret court known as the Star Chamber and the Sons and Daughters of Liberty in exchange for a reduced sentence. Is that correct?"

Baldwin looked at his attorney before speaking. "That's correct," he responded. "Here's what I'm offering. I'll explain how the Star Chamber was formed, how it worked, and how the SDL carried out our verdict."

Stevenson looked at Jeannie and Ismail, inviting them to speak if they wished. "I think you have to be a little more specific," Jeannie said. "We already have a lot of information about the Star Chamber and the SDL." Jeannie hoped that her bluffing would get Baldwin upset, at which point he may blurt out something they did not know, for free.

Instead, Baldwin laughed and leaned farther back into his chair. "I doubt that, Agent Loomis. I assume you and your colleagues raided the estate where the court held its sessions and found nothing. And, from what I heard, your only connection with the SDL was a now dead member. How am I doing?" he asked with a smirk on his face.

Jeannie did not respond until she could think of a different tactic. "Look, your honor. For several months there has been no Star Chamber activity. Perhaps your members have decided to terminate the court, in which case the investigation will, over time, become cold. If you want to play cat and mouse with us, I see no need to play since nothing is happening. Should the Star Chamber start up again, the investigation will resume. Do you have time on your hands to wait until that happens?"

Jeannie's reference to Baldwin's former title seemed to boost his ego, however temporary, but one could tell he was processing what Jeannie said, especially her reference to how much time he had left, being in his early seventies.

Baldwin looked at Stevenson, then Jeannie and Ismail, and finally leaned forward and whispered something into his attorney's ear. "My client would like to talk to me in private before we proceed if that is OK?" he asked, looking at the federal prosecutor.

"How much time do you need," Stevenson asked.

"No more than 10-minutes," came the response. Stevenson, Jeannie and Ismail returned to the smaller office where they first met.

"You seemed to strike a chord, Loomis. I think he might rollover now. How did you know that hitting him about his age would work?" Stevenson asked.

"I just figured that he's looking at what, a minimum fifteen to twenty years? That's almost a death sentence for him. That means many years behind bars where he can't molest young boys and girls."

"Do you think he's really going to give up anything useful, or is he just pulling our chain?" Ismail asked, looking at Jeannie.

"I wish I knew, but he's the one who asked for the audience with us," Jeannie replied. There was a knock on the door and upon opening it, there stood

Kaufman. "Good job, Agent Loomis. Your use of a little psychology worked. My client is willing to cooperate with you."

Jeannie, Ismail and Stevenson followed Kaufman back into the room with Baldwin. Baldwin stared at Jeannie and Ismail, and then said, "Agent Loomis, you said something to the effect that the Star Chamber is out of service as well as the SDL. You're correct regarding the Star Chamber, but you mean the great FBI hasn't connected the dots about the most recent deaths of two other judges? Specifically Judges Swartz and Kanamoto? The SDL is still very active. What are my taxes paying for?" he asked smiling.

Jeannie looked at Ismail and then back at Baldwin. "Do you want to expand on your statement or shall we continue to play your Ask A Question And If I Feel Like It I'll Respond game?" Jeannie asked, returning a smirk smile.

"Very well. I guess when you leave you'll get all the gory details. Let me start from the beginning, shall we. The Star Chamber has been in session for over two years. Agent Loomis, you are already aware of one of the most recent actions. In fact, your investigation caused the Seattle Police Department to reclassify an accidental death as a homicide.

"The former Secretary of State, Virginia McKenzie, correct?" Jeannie said.

"Exactly," Baldwin replied.

"That was the work of the SDL?" she asked. Baldwin nodded.

"Also, do you two recall a drone attack on a mountain top chateau in the Swiss Alps? The one in which Horace Beaumont and his entire family were killed by VX gas?" Baldwin asked again.

"I heard about it," said Ismail. "You are saying it was the SDL again?"

"Yes," said Baldwin and continued. "Agent Loomis, did you and your colleagues on the Seattle Police force actually think that the SDL member that brilliantly killed Daniel Blackstone and Summer Tillson, the radical attorney at the roadside café, was the only member of the SDL? Too bad he died before he could give you more information."

Jeannie's mind was in overdrive, and then it clicked. "So, what you're saying is that some SDL members are now, for whatever reason, killing judges who sat on the Star Chamber?"

"Not for some unknown reason," Baldwin laughed. "It's simply revenge! Let me spell it out for you so you and your partner there can understand. When I was active in the Star Chamber, the SDL had nine members that I was aware of. They were both in the United States and abroad. Our sergeant-at-arms was their leader. He selected them, and after a verdict was rendered chose who would carry out our sentence."

"So, you acted as both the judge and executioner?" asked Ismail.

Baldwin pressed one index finger to the other forming a teepee. He leaned forward and looked directly at Ismail. "Yes, we all did, Agent Flores."

"And the name of the sergeant-at-arms is?" Jeannie asked.

"Joey. Don't ask me his last name. I don't think any of us knew it, but I could be wrong. What I do know is that he served two tours of duty in the Middle East, Iraq and Afghanistan if memory serves. He was in a black ops unit, very classified. The original judge who came up with the concept of the Star Chamber recruited him since he shared the same values as we did. If you like, I can talk about that," Baldwin said.

"What's the name of that judge?" Ismail asked.

"Sorry Agent Flores, that's not part of the agreement," Baldwin quickly asserted. "Joey was given free reign by the first magistrate to recruit other members and carry out sentencing however he so chose. But, after my arrest, the Star Chamber panicked and ordered not only the court to go dark temporality, but to get rid of any loose ends, which meant that members of the SDL had to be eliminated. Three were killed almost immediately. One was responsible for killing the former Secretary of State, and the other two participated in the roadside café poisoning and drone attack. Who the Star Chamber used to commit those assassination, I don't know since I was out of commission. If they went after Joey, I guess they weren't successful. Joey obviously learned of his recruits being killed, and vanished with five other members."

"You said that Joey shared the Star Chamber judges' ideas. Can you explain that?" Jeannie asked.

"Sure, Agent Loomis. I'd be glad too," Baldwin responded. "Joey was the only SDL member who regularly attended court sessions. During breaks, he and I would occasionally talk. He's a very bright and articulate young man. I think he would've made a good jurist. Sorry, I digress. He was of the opinion that liberals in our society have been allowed to occupy government offices in our major cities such Los Angeles, San Francisco, Baltimore, New York and so on, where they install their socialist ideologies and contaminate those cities. Joey expressed his concerns about those cities having two types of law enforcement. One was for the rich and middle class since they had money, and the other was for those perceived to not have any. He said the last time he was in Los Angeles, for example, many of the downtown streets were filled with the homeless who crapped and urinated on the streets and sidewalks, yet no one is cited or arrested." Ismail remembered the male who defecated in front of him and Pinheiro just that day. "Mixed in with the homeless are street vendors cooking their food or selling merchandise on the sidewalks totally unregulated. No code enforcement is taking place by the city. Why? They don't have any money. But, a soccer mom driving her daughter to soccer practice in her Lexus gets pulled over for going thirty-four in a twenty-five mile-per-hour zone. Again why? Because she's perceived to have money. The police don't like it, but they have to go along with the cities' socialists' policies or lose their jobs. So, Joey and his recruits that made up the SDL had no qualms about carrying out our sentences like Secretary McKenzie, Beaumont and others."

"Who decided on where the Star Chamber meets?" Jeannie asked.

"That was up to Joey. He had all the judges' burner phones and notified them as to the location. He scheduled us to arrive at different times, supposedly so we wouldn't run into each other during our arrivals or departures and learn each other's identity, but we eventually learned the names of fellow judges, even calling their last names during calls for their verdict. You know, Judge Swartz, guilty. Judge Kanamoto, guilty. And so on.

"Do you know how Judge Swartz and Kanamoto were killed" Jeannie asked.

"No. The rumor mill inside this facility isn't reliable. Sometimes we don't get any new news.

Quickly, and hoping to trip up Baldwin, Jeannie asked, "And the names of the other remaining judges are?" acting as if she were about to write their names down on a piece of paper. "Nice try, Agent Loomis. Again, it's not part of the plea bargain. But, I would like to add something about Joey. Don't underestimate him, his IQ is off the charts. The military offered him a position in Army Intelligence if he would re-enlist, but he turned them down. I also heard that the CIA tried to recruit him before he went into the military, but again, that is only a rumor. When you think you have him, he'll surprise you by being one step ahead."

Additional questions did nothing to further the investigation and the meeting was preparing to break up, but Baldwin did not want to pass up the opportunity to pour vinegar into Jeannie's wound which he believed was still fresh. "Agent Loomis, I'm so sorry you were shot and lost your baby. I had nothing to do with that," he said with no hint of empathy. Jeannie felt the hurt but did not let on. "I would like to give you some information that I believe you and Agent Flores have wondered about for a long time. Who provided the layout of your Roseville substation? As a parting gift I'll give you that individual's name." Baldwin waited for the right moment and finally said, "Your former SAC, Davenport, provided a lot of information to the Star Chamber when he was alive."

Jeannie and Ismail shook hands with Stevenson. "I hope the information he gave you helps your investigation," he said.

"I think we got enough to re-open the case on the Star Chamber. How much time do you think he'll get after the plea bargain?" Jeannie asked.

"He's still going to serve at least ten-years in federal prison, but once others incarcerated there find out he's a pedophile, who knows what will happen to him."

Ismail and Jeannie got into the elevator. "Did Baldwin get too good of a deal?" Ismael asked.

"No, I think we got a lot of good information, but I'm not sure if we have anything concrete enough for a follow-up. I'll fill in Lomax when we get back and give this information to Burk and Darcy, but we need to keep our focus on Hassan."

Chapter Eleven

"Unit one, the suspect is on the move, walking west on Oak Street. We have two agents following him." Pinheiro reported from the bureau car driven by Jeannie.

"Roger that, unit one."

"Foot-surveillance team, remember that he already burnt the stakeout team in Dallas. Keep a loose tail and if you lose him, don't worry about it since we know where he lives," Pinheiro further advised.

Hassan's walk was uneventful. He bought something to eat and drink from a street vendor and walked back to his apartment. "Unit one, the subject has returned to his residence," Pinheiro said, and turning to Jeannie continued, "Shit! This could go on forever. We need to flush him out and see if he's the real deal that Dallas felt he was."

"How are we going to do that?" Jeannie asked.

"Let's go back to your office," Pinheiro replied. "I want to check in with Amir and see what the most recent emails from Hassan say. You might as well call my cousin in also. I think Hassan will stay in his apartment and hopefully get online."

Joey had everyone meet in the living room. The same piece of cardboard showing the Pavlenko's residence layout used the previous night was resting on a cheap easel. "We'll hit the house tomorrow night. I'll schedule an afternoon meeting with Pavlenko. Then close to our scheduled time, I'll call him and say I'm running late, but that I really need to get his input about our plans for disrupting the upcoming Presidential fundraiser. He hates the President so much that I know he'll be eager to hear our plans. The butler will have already left for the day.

"Once I'm in the house, Amy and Billy will stroll hand-in-hand past the front of the place, waiting for the two security guards to come out and do their normal perimeter check. You two, Sandi and Vicki, will be here—pointing to the neighboring house on the sketch--hiding in the shadows," Joey continued, pointing at Chico. "No one reacts until you see my flashlight from the third-floor window. Understood?" Everyone acknowledged Joey's order.

"Once I'm with Pavlenko, I'll ask see the Romanoff jewels. If he has them out on his desk like he did the last time I was there, we've got it made. If not, I'll get him to open the safe. Once the safe is open, I'll eliminate him and then take out the security officer in the monitoring room. That leaves one security personnel left. I'll track him down as if I'm about to leave, like I've done several times before. Once he's dead, I'll go to the third-floor and send the signal. At that point you three, Chico, Sandi and Vicki, come out of the shadows and eliminate the two guards outside. I'll then open the front door so you three, plus Billy and Amy, can drag the two dead guards into the house.

"Vicki, you and Sandi try to destroy anything in the surveillance room that might connect us. Billy, Chico and Amy, you'll meet me upstairs where I'll be collecting the jewelry and money from the safe. Take anything else you see that appears valuable. Vicki, when you and Sandi are through in the room, start on the bottom floor and collect anything you feel we can use. Money, drugs, anything. We'll all meet on the second floor to give it a once over. We should only be in the house for twenty-minutes max, and then off we go. Any questions? Alright, we'll leave here at nine-thirty, take the van and--pointing again at the sketch--park it here. Billy and Amy will be the first ones to get out, followed by me after I make the phone call. You three need to wait until you see me enter the house before taking your positions. If by chance the two guards come outside earlier than normal to check the perimeter, you two--pointing to Amy and Billy--

have to really get it on with each other so the guards will want to watch. Got it?" Joey asked.

"Got it," Billy said with Amy nodding.

"Alright, let's check our weapons, suppressors and gloves. Let's go people," Joey said as if he could hardly wait for the adventure.

As soon as Amir saw Pinheiro and Jeannie, he motioned for them to come in and look at the translation of his online conversation with Hassan on the monitoring screen. Hassan boastfully told Amir that American intelligence had fucked up their surveillance in Dallas, allowing him to escape capture. Amir congratulated him, inflating Hassan's ego. "Do you have a clean phone?" Amir asked.

"Yes, I have two burner phones," Hassan's answered.

"Good, " Amir said. "Give me one of the numbers so I can call you tomorrow and set up a meeting time. We can formulate your plans then, that is if you still want to carry through with your jihad." An irritated Hassan stated that he was more motivated than before, and wished to get on with it or he would have to find someone else that could help him. He then complied and gave Amir the number for one of the burner phones. Hassan stopped the transcribed conversation at that point.

"Can you trace burner phones?" Ismail asked as he entered the room, catching the last part of the transcription on Amir's screen.

"Yes," said Burk.

"The carrier can," added Darcy. "They can trace any device that's actively on their network, whether they have GPS or not. The method is called Network-based tracking. The more accurate type is Advanced Forward Link-Trilateration followed by Cell Tower Triangulation." Darcy blushed when she realized that a simple yes, would have sufficed.

Ismail looked at Pinheiro and said, "OK, now I know where you're going with this. If Hassan carries either of the burner phones when he's out and about, the foot-surveillance team can have a looser tail, since the GPS will inform us as to his location if he gives them the slip. Nice!" Pinheiro got a big grin on his face and said, "How can anyone doubt that we're related. Two great minds."

"Oh God, give us a break," Jeannie said while Darcy and Burk looked at each other and laughed.

Lomax entered the room as the laughter subsided. "I've ordered Subway sandwiches and they should be here soon. Why don't we go into the briefing room?" he suggested.

As the group trekked to the briefing room, Amir grabbed Pinheiro's arm and motioning for him to hold back saying, "He's ready to explode. Sorry for the pun."

"I know. I have a plan, but I need to run it pass the FBI legal team. Jeannie," Pinheiro called out, causing Jeannie to stop in her tracks and turn. "Is there a way you can request that someone from your legal department meet us here in the break room as soon as possible?"

"Sure," Jeannie answered. "I'll call them right now. By the way, make sure you keep the SAC in the loop. He has a lot of powerful friends in D.C."

"Good to know," Pinheiro said as he blew Jeannie an invisible kiss which she grabbed with her hand.

Colleen Day from legal showed up while everyone was finishing their sandwiches. "Gee, guess I'm late," she said.

"Not at all," Lomax said, offering her any of the remaining sandwiches, chips and soft drinks. She helped herself while Pinheiro introduced himself, stating he was with the Department of Homeland Security.

"Wow, must be big," she said. Pinheiro gave her a synopsis of past and present events. "We understand that currently, with what we have, we wouldn't be able to successfully obtain an arrest warrant."

"Yes, you're correct," Day said matter-of-factly.

"OK, here's what I'm suggesting, Ms. Day."

"Please, call me Colleen," she said.

"OK, Colleen, here's what we hope to accomplish." Walking to the white-board and grabbing a dry erase marker, Pinheiro wrote the number one followed by a hyphen and continued, "It's time for Hassan to reveal his true intentions beyond the rhetoric he has shared with Amir on-line and at the hotel. We'll set up another meet similar to what your Dallas field office arranged. We have two rooms set up at a hotel downtown. Amir will continue to act as Hassan's al Qaeda mentor, promising the tools he'll need for the jihad while agents listen and record in the neighboring room. He'll show him photos of previously used large truck bombs and assorted handguns that should force Hasson to select the tools he wants. Amir will ask him if he's chosen a specific target in the city." Everyone looked at each other; Day stood still with her mouth agape.

"You really aren't going to give this terrorist a bomb, are you?" Day asked.

"No, this is strictly to meet the requirements we need for appropriate search warrants and to know, once and for all, how dedicated Hassan is to committing his jihad.

"If Hassan performs as you hope he does, you'll have easily met the burden of proof, and I think any jury will see that the motivation to kill came from him, not a federal law enforcement agency. I would easily sign off on this," Day said while taking a sip of coffee.

Joey showed up at Pavlenko's residence as he had done before. One of the security officers opened the front door, gave him a quick once over and allowed him to enter. Had the officer decided to frisk Joey and discovered his weapon, Joey was prepared to react. Instead the security guard closed the door and walked over to the side of the entry and continued to watch a TV program with his partner. Joey made note of their location and proceeded upstairs. Two security officers were looking at the monitoring equipment on the second-floor and did not raised their heads as Joey walked by. By that time, Billy and Amy should have been strolling hand-in-hand on the sidewalk in front of the residence, and Chico, Sandi and Vicki should have been in the shadows.

Joey entered the room and saw Pavlenko working out on a NordicTrak treadmill. *Be nice if you just died while working out, you fat fuck--but then I couldn't get you to open the safe,* Joey thought. He established eye contact with Pavlenko.

"Joey, great job over in Berkeley. Your people did a good job shaking things up. I hear they had to cancel the show. Wonderful, wonderful! I hope you have something special for the President next month," he said as he slowed the treadmill and prepared to dismount. Once the machine stopped, he grabbed a towel and began wiping the sweat off his face. "Would you like some water?" he asked as he helped himself to a bottle of Acqua di Cristallo which Joey knew cost $60,000 per 750 ml.

"No, thank you," Joey replied. "I wanted to discuss plans for the President's fundraiser and give you a quote about how much I think it will cost."

"Yes, yes. Not a problem. I want it big and bad so all media outlets will have to broadcast it. Hurt some people, set some fires, make it big," Pavlenko said as he walked to his desk chair.

Joey outlined his plan and Pavlenko liked it. "I think I'll need about fifty-thousand dollars to set it up," he said. Pavlenko started to open his side desk drawn where Joey knew he kept some cash, but as Joey had hoped by requesting such a large sum, Pavlenko changed his mind and opened the safe.

Pulling his silenced semi-automatic from the back of his waistband, Joey fired one round into Pavlenko's knee while placing his hand over Pavlenko's mouth to prevent a scream for help. He told Pavlenko he would be killed if he did not write down the combination to the gun vault. Pavlenko looked up at Joey and knew that if he did not comply, he would be killed. Grimacing in pain, he reached for his pen on the desk and wrote the combination. Facing away from Joey he never saw Joey pull the trigger that fired a round into the back of his head. He banged his head into the safe's door before falling on the floor. Joey took a quick look in the safe, saw the jewelry and two large stacks of bills. Turning, he headed down to the second floor where he found the two interior guards looking at the monitoring equipment and talking. As they turned to look at Joey, it was too late. Two quick bursts from Joey's weapon hit the guards in their chests. He finished them off with two head shots. Returning to the third-floor study, he turned on the small flashlight he had in his front pocket and pointed it out the window.

Vicki and Sandi saw the light and started toward the guard walking from their side of the house. Chico saw them, advanced, and did the same from his side. With little effort they took the last two guards by surprise and killed them. Chico was able to single-handedly pull his downed guard to the front door, then helped Vicki and Sandi pull their much heavier victim near the front of the house and left him on the sidewalk until they could get Chico's guard into the house. Joey opened the front door and helped Chico with the first body. They returned and pulled in the second.

"OK, let's start searching the areas you were assigned," Joey said as he began his return to the third-floor. In the safe he found in excess of $150,000 plus a handgun and the Romanoff jewelry he had seen a few days earlier. Grabbing a pillow case from Pavlenko's bed, he bagged the cash followed by the jewelry. Chico found a gun vault containing so many weapons the group had to make two trips to get them all to the van. Pavlenko had AK-47s, AR 15s, assorted semi-automatics and a ton of ammunition. Vicki and Sandi destroyed the recording equipment and felt that nothing useable was left for law enforcement. They decided that the cash, jewelry and weapons were enough of a haul, so other valuable items were left behind. In twenty-five minutes the group was out of the house.

Chapter Twelve

Two days later, an excited Hassan arrived at the Hilton Hotel in the financial district, again using a Lyft driver. Amir answered the knock and invited him to enter. Hassan had previously listed several of his possible targets online, all located in that part of the city. He focused on the financial infrastructure of the United States, expressing that a successful attack on any of the targeted financial institutions would cause the U.S. economy to implode. He wanted a bomb big enough to bring down a building similar to those destroyed on 9-11, but he had neither the knowledge to build a bomb nor the financial backing to purchase one. Pinheiro, Jeannie, and Ismael were in the adjacent room with the transcriber. Amir had to walk a virtual tightrope when he said that al Qaeda would provide the truck bomb, making sure the suggestion first came from Hassan. Amir was careful to never be the first to suggest violence, always giving Hassan a way out.

Initially, Hassan said he wanted to hit multiple targets, similar to what he had seen al Qaeda do in the Middle East. He talked about placing backpacks at airports, shopping malls, and sporting events, and setting them off with a cellphone. Then he paused and took out a folded piece of paper from his rear pocket and said, "First, I want to bring this building down." It was a skyscraper housing one of the nation's largest credit card and banking institutions. "I will park a truck inside here--pointing to the underground garage--and once I am clear, I will remotely detonate the bomb. I need a big bomb to bring the building down. I do not want something to happen like the first bombing of the World Trade Center.

"My brother," said Amir, "My superiors feel you should concentrate on one large target first so you will tie up the American police resources. Then, while they are investigating the bombing of this building, you can hit your other targets." Hassan agreed, saying again and again that he wanted to impress the new leader of al Qaeda.

"Here are some pictures of truck bombs we have used in both Iraq and Afghanistan," said Amir, who passed two photos over to Hassan.

Hassan quickly pointed to both pictures and said, "This is what I need. When can you get me the truck bomb?"

Pinheiro anticipated this request and told Amir to tell Hassan that a bomb this big would take one-week to build. Hassan did not seem disappointed, but asked how he should do it. Amir suggested that once the bomb was made and secured in the back of a truck, the two of them could meet. He asked Hassan if he had a car? Hassan quickly said he would get one. "Fine," said Amir. "It will take our brothers one week to build such a bomb. After you get a car, find the directions to the San Francisco zoo by Golden Gate Park. I will call you and tell you where I am parked with the truck once it is ready. You can take whatever route you want to your target and I will follow to pick you up once you have it parked." Hassan had a huge smile on his face shaking his head excitedly up and down. His dream of jihad was almost ready. He shook Amir's hand and quickly left the hotel.

Per Lomax's request, Pinheiro contacted both the FBI's own bomb squad, the SFPD tactical team, and the U.S. Army, requesting that their best bomb technicians meet at the bureau the following day. They discussed how to create a non-destructive bomb big enough to impress Hassan who might have some knowledge about the type of bomb needed to bring down a building of that size. Working almost nonstop, the bomb experts began assembling the device.

Amir told Pinheiro that he had an additional idea that should cement any conviction of Hassan once he was taken into custody. He would suggest to Hassan that he should make a video recording his desire for jihad, which upon successful detonation of the device would be sent to the new al Qaeda leader. Pinheiro felt it was an excellent idea. Meeting two days later, Hassan sat in front of a video camera operated by Amir with a cloth wrapped around his face, showing only his eyes. For seventeen-minutes Hassan told his intended Middle East audience how proud he was to be an al Qaeda soldier and took credit for the attack he would soon unleash on America.

Five days later Hassan drove a cheap used Ford Focus to the San Francisco Zoo, parking on Sloat Blvd. He saw Amir standing by the side of a truck parked far away from other vehicles, and Ami's car parked behind the truck. When he approached Amir, Pinheiro and Ismael were parked across the street in a van equipped with a two-way mirror on its side. With them was an agent recording the meeting who could also interpret what was being said. Amir looked up and down the street and then pulled up the tarp covering the truck's bed. Hassan's eye became wide and he broke into a huge smile. The bomb covered the entire bed of the truck and looked extremely real, even to Amir. He handed Hassan a cellphone telling him the number needed for detonation. He and Hassan exchanged keys; Hassan climbed into the cab of the truck and Amir did the same with Hassan's vehicle.

Surveillance teams were advised that the jihadist suspect was now in the truck and tracking indicated he was moving toward his intended target. Ismail drove the bureau car parallel to Hassan on side streets; Jeannie did the same on the opposite side of the route with Pinheiro handling the radio.

Hassan arrived at his target and drove the truck inside a parking garage with Amir following. Finding a parking spot in the middle of the lot, he parked, got out of the truck, locked the doors with the key fob, and proceeded to the passenger side of Amir's vehicle and got in. Amir drove Hassan to the rooftop parking of a building across from the credit card building from which Hassan could see his jihad take place. He thought it would provide him with a perfect view of the blast and subsequent destruction once he dialed the number, not noticing there were several occupied cars already parked there.

Hassan and Amir quickly jumped out of the car. Hassan looked across the street at his target and pulled the cellphone from his pocket, and smiling at Amir dialed the number and pressed "send." Nothing happened. He pressed "send" again and got the same result. Again, he tried, not noticing that seven individuals dressed in black and heavily armed with assault rifles were running toward him. "Get down, get down," he heard as he turned and saw the FBI tactical team advance on them. Hassan, still holding the cellphone and repeatedly pressing the "send" button was taken to the ground next to Amir, still pressing the "send" button until his hands were placed behind his back and he was cuffed. Pinheiro walked up, and with a gloved hand picked up the cellphone.

Approaching Pinheiro, Jeannie said, "Congratulations, Washington will be impressed." Before he could respond, Ismail yelled, "Hey, what about me. I helped a little bit, and if medals are going to be awarded, I want one." Laughing with Jeannie, Ricky said, "That's my cousin!"

Chapter Thirteen

Everyone at the San Francisco bureau celebrated with Pinheiro, Ismael, and Jeannie as they returned to the office. "Great job!" Lomax said, shaking Pinheiro's hand. "Couldn't have done it without your team, sir," Pinheiro responded. "Debriefing can wait until tomorrow morning, say ten a.m. I'll have media relations write up something if they're contacted by the press. I think the way it went down, they have no clue. OK. I'll see everyone tomorrow."

Walking to the garage elevator, Ismail had them laughing when he described Hassan repeatedly pushing the "send button." "It reminded me of all those Roadrunner cartoons. You know, Wile E. Coyote. He sees the Roadrunner coming and, at what he thinks is the precise moment, he pushes down on the plunger to detonate the Acme Dynamite and nothing happens. He does it over and over, just like

Hassan did with the phone. I mean, I'll never forget his pushing as hard as he could on the button as our guys swooped down on him."

Reaching their cars, Ismael saw Ricky head toward the passenger side of Jeannie's sportscar and yelled more for Jeannie's benefit than Pinheiro, "Hey, you two, don't do anything that I'll be doing when I get home."

"God, I hope when you get home, Bianca has a headache," Jeannie said.

"Not going to happen," Ismael retorted. "Once I take off my clothes and she sees this USDA prime body, she can't resist."

"Goodnight Ismael," Jeannie said while shaking her head.

"Good night boss, goodnight cuz," Ismail replied as they drove their cars out of the garage. "Hungry?" Ricky asked as he put his head on the headrest and closed his eyes.

"Yes. And you?" Jeannie answered.

"Yeah. You know, Ismail told me of a great restaurant in the city called, Uma Casa on Church Street. Maybe we can go there."

"Why am I not surprised that Ismael recommended one of the best Portuguese restaurants in the city? Sure, that sounds like fun," she said, making an illegal U-turn.

When they arrived, Jeannie was surprised to find an available table in the corner. "Gee, this is nice," she said as they sat, not noticing the host wink at Ricky. He ordered a Sangria Vermehlo; Jeannie ordered a white port. On the other side of the dining room three guitar players made music for the diners. Fortunately, it was not too noisy for Ricky and Jeannie to comfortably visit. Jeannie raised her glass and toasted Ricky for a job well done.

"You too," he said, as they clang their glasses together. After a sip of her wine, Jeannie excused herself to visit the ladies' room. When she returned, she picked up her glass and was about to take another sip when she saw something on the bottom of the glass. A diamond engagement ring. She looked at Ricky and back at the ring, then started to cry. "Oh God, here we go with the Hallmark moment thing," Ricky said, as he pulled out his handkerchief and handed it to her. "I'm too tired to get down on my knees, but will you marry me?" he asked. Jeannie did not reply but instead placed her fingers into the wine glass and fished out the ring. She then handed it to him, causing him to feel she was going to refuse. "What, are you saying no?" he asked.

"No, you fool, you need to put it on my finger. And yes, I will marry you." On cue, the three guitarists came over to their table and played a song that neither Jeannie nor Ricky would ever recall.

The next morning, they awoke in Jeannie's bed to knocking on the front door. They grabbed their cellphones to see if perhaps they had missed an incoming call. Neither had. Jeannie and Ricky dressed quickly. Jeannie put on a robe hanging of the inside of the master bathroom door and Ricky put on his sweatpants and t-shirt. Both grabbed their guns and headed downstairs were someone was persistently knocking on the door. Jeannie opened the door with Ricky standing by her side, both hiding their handgun behind their back.

"Oh, you're home. I was so worried. I saw on Fox and Friends this morning that you two arrested a terrorist in San Francisco. My word, what's the world coming too?" asked Delores, still in curlers. "Oh, how rude of me. Hello Mr. Pinheiro. How are you?" Delores asked blushing and again, absentmindedly touching her curlers.

"We're fine Delores. So, it's already on the news?" Jeannie asked.

"Oh yes, on all the stations, but I only watch Fox News. I can't stand those other fake news channels. Well, I don't want to impose so I'd better get home. I just wanted to make sure you were safe. Bye!" And with that, the neighborhood queen of gossip and watchdog walked back to her house.

Jeannie closed the door while Ricky broke into deep, rich and infectious laughter. Jeannie laughed along with him, causing them both to cry so hard that tears formed in their eyes. Jeannie wrapped her arms around Ricky and the laughter got even louder. "Oh, my God!" Jeannie said.

"What"? replied Ricky.

"I hope she didn't see my engagement ring. If she did, everyone in the neighborhood will know by lunchtime, guaranteed. They looked at each other and broke out in laughter again.

Chapter Fourteen

"So, these items used to belong to the last Czar of Russia, huh?" asked Vicki, who next to Joey was the most intelligent member of the group, having attended college almost non-stop since graduating early from high school.

"That's what Pavlenko told me," said Joey. "He said that back in 1922 they were estimated to be worth north of five-hundred million." Everyone looked at the Romanoff jewelry, but most were concentrating on their share of the cash taken from Pavlenko's safe which totaled $150,000, or $25,000 apiece. Joey divided the money and gave everyone their equal share. "Everyone happy?" he asked, not expecting a negative response--and none came. "Enjoy, but tomorrow we continue with our mission of revenge for our slain comrades and my plan for the Sadler affair, SLA style."

Jeannie and Ismail caught up with the SAC and Pinheiro in the briefing room. Jeannie grabbed a leftover soda and half of a sandwich; Ismail took bottled water. "How did it go?" Lomax asked.

"Lots of information to fill-in the blanks about the Star Chamber investigation, but nothing concrete to act on immediately. He was our main threat," Jeannie said, pointing to Hassan's picture on the white-board.

Lomax continued, "I agree, but I need to pull Ismail off for a few hours to liaison with the SFPD. While you two were at the plea-bargain meeting, they responded to multiple homicides at Anatoly Pavlenko's mansion in Pacific Heights. Five dead, including Pavlenko himself. It looks like a professional hit. Flores, I told them you'd be there as soon as you returned from your meeting."

"Yes sir," Ismail responded and headed out of the briefing room.

"FBI Agent Flores," Ismail said to a stationed SFPD officer as he walked toward the crime scene tape. The officer logged Ismail's name into his logbook and lifted up the tape.

"Flores," shouted Paul Freeman, a long-time homicide detective who had known Ismail for years.

Ismail approached and said shaking hands, "Heard you got a big one."

"Actually, it couldn't have happened to a better guy, "Detective Freeman said. Ismail pulled a pair of latex gloves from his pocket while Freeman handed him covers for his feet. While putting the protective coverings on, Freeman said, "Five bodies in the house, but we found signs of someone having been dragged and a trail of blood from the outside into the foyer. Pavlenko's body is on the third floor. Two security guards got hit in the security monitoring room which, by the way, was trashed. You'll see the first two right inside the front door lying on the marble floor."

Freeman opened the door, and immediately Ismail saw two middle-aged white males who looked Russian laying face up with entry wounds in the center of their foreheads. "Each took one in the chest and a coup de grace shot to make sure they were dead. Let me tell you how I see it before we do the walkthrough, and see if you agree," Freeman said. "These two got it outside. I think it had to have happened after events in the house, otherwise the monitoring crew would have seen it. Someone had to have already gained entrance and later opened the front door."

"Hey, is that a Renoir?" asked Ismail pointing to a picture hanging on the wall accented by lights.

"Flo, I didn't know you were an art aficionado," replied Freeman. "But, you're right. It's the real deal worth about twenty-five million. The thing is, it was stolen by the Nazis in World War II and had never been seen again until it turned up here. If you like that one, wait until you see the art on display in the rest of the mansion."

Reaching the second floor, Freeman took Ismail to the monitoring room where two more bodies were located. "This guy took two in the chest and was standing when he got hit. The guy seated has two headshots, one in the forehead and one behind his right ear. We haven't found any brass, so whoever did this must have collected the spent shells," Freeman said.

On the third floor, Ismail saw another Renoir and paintings by Raphael and Hans Memling. "Stolen by the Nazis also?" Ismail asked.

"Yep," came Freeman's response. "Over there's a bust dating back to the time of Cleopatra." Ismail saw the open wall safe and Pavlenko's body lying on the floor. Whatever contents the safe guarded was long gone.

"Wonder how much was inside here?" Ismail asked.

"Wait 'till you see what we believe is missing in the next room," replied Freeman as he escorted Ismail through the door. The room had been a dedicated exercise room with numerous pieces of exercise equipment. Instantly, Ismail focused on a large state of the art gun vault with its doors open. Whatever might have resided inside had been cleaned out. "This is the Sportsman double-wide series gun vault capable of holding 12 assault rifles, maybe AKs since he was Russian, nine pistols or semis, and 4-5 high powered sporting rifles. Dust on the floor shows the outline of what we think were ammo boxes," Freeman explained.

"Just what we need. A bunch of killers with better firepower than we have," Ismail said.

"Look at this view," Freeman said walking out onto the rooftop terrace off the exercise room. "Pavlenko had a million-dollar view. Probably more than that. He had this place on the market for a little while, dropping the price from forty-six million to thirty-four," Freeman said. "Hell, when it's not foggy, he could have seen Alcatraz Island."

"Motive?" asked Ismail.

"Greed, revenge. Shit, who knows. A guy as wealthy as him, I'm sure has a lot of enemies."

"Can we go back to the monitoring room?" Ismail asked.

"Be my guest," Freeman answered as they went down one floor.

It appeared to Ismail that someone removed computer hard drives in addition to trashing the place and said, "I was hoping that maybe they'd slipped up and left something behind that our forensic computer team could analyze, but apparently they knew what they were doing."

"You know Ismail, they did forget to thoroughly check his desk. He had a hidden drawer, and unless someone really searched thoroughly, it wouldn't be found. We did, and found his laptop, but it's encrypted."

"Hey. If you fill out a Chain of Evidence sheet, I can take it back to our geek squad and let them try to break in," Esmail said. "They were able to crack Judge Baldwins computer in the Star Chamber case."

"Great," said Freeman, calling out to someone named Virgil. "Bring over the laptop and a Chain of Evidence form, will you?"

"Thanks, Esmail said. "I'll let you know if they're able to get in, and what, if anything, is found."

"Hope you do, since right now I've got squat, and the press will be all over us soon," Freeman replied.

Pinheiro walked into Jeannie's office carrying two cups of coffee. "Thought you might need this," he said while yawning. "Yeah, I do. Someone kept me awake most of the night," she said, grabbing the cup.

Just then, Darcy and Burk entered Jeannie's office. "Hey guys, I have something for you to work on now that we've cleared the DHS terrorist's case."

"Oh, that hurts," Pinheiro said laughing. "But, I have to admit, if it weren't for the FBI's help, God knows what could have happened. "I can leave you three alone if you want," he said. "No, that's OK. Maybe you might have some thoughts about how we should proceed with the new information Baldwin gave Ismail and me. It's about the Star Chamber case," Jeannie said.

Before Jeannie could brief Burk and Darcy, Ismail arrived carrying Pavlenko's laptop and evidence chain document. "Hey, you guys having a party and I didn't get invited?" he asked.

"How bad was it at Pavlenko's house?" Jeannie asked.

"Whoever whacked him and his security team knew what they were doing," Ismail said. Looking at Burk and Darcy, he continued, "I have something for you two. It's Pavlenko's laptop, but it's encrypted. The SFPD found it in the secret drawer of his desk. I volunteered you two experts and they gladly accepted our help. Here's the evidence log."

Darcy took the laptop from Ismail and turned her attention back to Jeannie. "I know this is a shot in the dark, but Ismail and I got some new information from Baldwin." She, along with Ismail, filled in Burk and Darcy with the latest from the disgraced judge. "Not much to go on," said Burk. "Someone named Joey, white male, in his thirties, former military, black ops in the Army."

"I know. Ismail, can you come farther in and close the door?" Jeannie asked. Ismail did as Jeannie requested and returned his attention to her. "What I'm going to tell you stays in this room." She quickly established eye contact with everyone including Pinheiro. "Baldwin told us that SAC Davenport was the one who provided the layout of our Roseville office and the staffing schedule when the place was hit by those three assholes."

"What? That fucker!" Darcy said, quickly feeling color flood into her cheeks. "Oh, I'm so sorry for swearing."

"No need to apologize, that's what that prick was," Ismail said. "Can you two work backward?

You know, check his computer usage, cellphone and bank records?

Maybe we'll get lucky," Jeannie said.

"With pleasure. Anything else?" Burk asked as he and Darcy prepared to leave Jeannie's office.

"No, that's all I've got. Jump on Pavlenko's computer first. If there's something that can help the SFPD, let's find it," Jeannie said as the two departed.

"Hey," said Pinheiro. Anyone else hungry?" he asked looking at this watch.

"I am," said Ismail, but if you two were planning on a nooner here in Jeannie's office, I'd understand."

"You're right!" Pinheiro said looking at Jeannie. "My cousin's a pervert." The three left, heading to the IHOP around the corner for lunch.

Ismail again congratulated both of them on their engagement. "I told you, boss, that once you have a Portuguee, you can't go back."

Jeannie laughed; but instead of a joking, she came back with, "So true," sporting a huge smile.

"The wifey wanted me to ask if there's a date set yet?" Ismail said.

"We just got engaged," Ricky quipped, smiling at Jeannie.

"What I'd like to do after we take the new information from Judge Baldwin as far as we can, is for the two of us to head up to my cabin in Coeur d' Alene and relax. Then we can make plans. What do you think?" Jeannie asked while leaning into Ricky, who nodded in agreement.

The next morning Ismail, Pinheiro, and Jeannie were in the briefing room removing Hassan investigation items from the white-board, sipping coffee and eating bagels. Lomax joined them briefly and asked Jeannie if there were any updates. She brought the SAC up to speed, even though there really was not much new information.

Ismail's cellphone rang. He glanced at the display and said it was Darcy. "Yeah Darcy, what's up?—pause--No shit! We're on our way." Ismail told Ricky and Jeannie that not only did Burk and Darcy get past the encryption, they found security files showing videos of all the murders. Pavlenko had been spying on his security staff.

Chapter Fifteen

"This warehouse should fit the bill," Joey said to Amy while sitting in a second car used by the group.

"Kind of shabby, don't you think," Amy said.

"Yeah, but it fits our purpose on two counts. First, after I re-establish contact with the remaining Star Chamber justices, explaining why I went into hiding, I'll suggest that for the first new court session we won't want to draw attention, and thus this warehouse. Secondly, I don't think the cops care about a place this shitty, so we should be able to come and go with the furniture from the last Star Chamber location and stage the warehouse before the court goes into session. OK, let's go, we need to stop at one more place," Joey said.

Jeannie, Pinheiro, and Ismael entered Darcy and Burk's computer lab. SAC Lomax was leaning over

Burk and Darcy's shoulders fixated on their large computer screen. "I can't believe it. It really shows the killings?" asked Ismail.

"Yes, it does, and his system also provides audio," Burk responded. Lomax backed away, allowing Ismael, Pinheiro, and Jeannie to view the screen more fully. Pressing a button, Burk filled the screen showing a male being allowed entrance to the mansion. The male is videoed going up floors until he reaches the third-floor where Pavlenko is seen exercising on a treadmill. "Joey, so nice to see you," he can be heard saying.

"Joey!" shouted Jeannie while looking at Ismail. "What are the odds?"

Pavlenko continued, "I've already transferred funds to your off-shore account for your next mission, my friend. This is only for you. I will give you whatever necessary funds you need for your recruitment exercise. I was very impressed in how you screwed up the U.C. event the other night. Very impressed. By the way, there is an upcoming event in the Senate over his impeachment. I want as many protestors as possible outside creating havoc with the police, calling for his downfall."

"Understood. You will not be disappointed," Joey said.

"This is the guy who's either the leader or one of Antifa's main go-to guys," said Pinheiro. "Now we have evidence of who sponsors their activities. Of course, it doesn't do us any good now that Pavlenko's dead."

"How is your side-job going Joey?" Pavlenko was heard asking.

"Side-job?" asked Joey.

"Yes, I see Judge Kanamoto died recently. Your handy work again, dah?" Pavlenko asked.

"Oh my God!" Jeannie said excitedly, turning to Ismail. He's part of the SDL and Star Chamber." Everyone watched Burk maneuver through various files he had imported from Pavlenko's laptop on to his. The outside video did not pick up anything other than the muffled shots from four killers, two males and three females seen coming out of the shadows, shooting the exterior guards who had no time to react.

Joey was seen entering the monitoring room and eliminating the two interior guards. Neither of them had a chance to clear their weapon. He was picked up again opening the front door and allowing the other five to enter. The rest of the video showed them systematically going floor to floor to collect valuables, and multiple trips to take all weapons from the gun vault.

No one in the room spoke while the files were being viewed. Silence was broken by Ismail saying he needed to contact Detective Freeman, that this was going to make his day. He left the room while reaching for his cellphone. Pinheiro looked at Lomax and made a suggestion. "We still don't know their identities, but I have an idea. With your permission, I'd like to connect

Darcy and Burk with a friend in the DOD," making reference to the Department of Defense.

"Go for it," responded Lomax.

Pinheiro dialed a number from his directory and waited a few seconds. "Hello, Miranda?" he asked. "Ricky Pinheiro here. Fine, fine and you?—pausing for her response—Great. Hey, I'm working a case with the FBI and the San Francisco Police Department. Yeah, the Pavlenko murders, how did you know? Already? Gee, when the media gets a hot story they're off and running before the bodies are cold. Listen, we found Pavlenko's laptop hidden in a secret desk drawer. Two of the FBI's finest--smiling at Darcy and Burk--got past his encryption and, get this, found security files with videos showing all of the killings with audio. No, I'm serious. About time we get some breaks, huh? Here's what I'm hoping you can do for us—pausing for her comments--Wow, two great minds think alike. Yes, I'll have the two FBI computer forensic members connect with you and they'll send you the files. Let me put Darcy on the line and you two can work out the details. I owe you Miranda, big time! OK, here's Darcy." With that he handed his phone to Darcy, and as she began talking to Miranda, Pinheiro turned to Lomax, Burk, and Jeannie and said, "Miranda and her team are experts in facial recognition. I'm having Darcy send the files of all suspects to her so she can run them through their various systems. Name a data bank and she can access it. DOD, Interpol, FAA, Passport control, it's amazing what she can find."

"How long do you think it'll take her?" asked Lomax.

"She'll probably get a hit quickly on this Joey character if it's true he was in the U.S. Army. DMV data should come up with most of the others if they ever had a driver's license or identification card," Pinheiro said.

"Hello, Judge Silverman? This is Joey. Yes, Joey, your former sergeant-at-arms. How are you?" Judge Silverman was a little suspicious and very cagey in his conversation. "I want to apologize for going into hiding, but understand that when the decision was made by you and your fellow magistrates to terminate the court temporarily, I naturally panicked and went underground so to speak—pause--Yes, I'm aware of Judge Swartz and Kanamoto's recent deaths. Sad since they had done such great work on the Star Chamber. Do you feel the other judges feel secure enough to start the court again, because if you are, I've found a temporary location and I can quickly have it set up for the court." Judge Silverman said that several of the judges had discussed starting up the Star Chamber again, and he sounded as if he were intrigued by Joey's proposal. He asked Joey to give him a few days and he would poll the other members of the court and get back to him. Joey felt that Silverman took the bait and would convince the other judges to meet.

Forty-five minutes later, Joey arrived at a small house located in Alameda. He parked in the driveway since parking was at a premium. The person he wanted to see rented a detached garage located to the rear and side of the main house as his residence. "Shalom," Joey said to a college-aged Arab male coming out of the side garage door. He saw Joey approach as he looked through the single garage window. "Shalom," came the reply as they reached out to shake hands. The Arab invited Joey into the sparsely furnished garage housing a small flat-screen television set, a used and open hide-a-bed, and a small kitchen table supporting a portable microwave. "Sit, sit. Would you like some tea?" he asked.

"Yes, that would be great," Joey answered.

"What brings you to me?" he asked, while pouring bottled water into a teapot and preparing two coffee cups.

"I need three bombs capable of leveling a twenty-five thousand square foot warehouse and incinerating everything inside. The bombs need to fit into three ceramic flower pots, ten and a half inches wide and sixteen inches tall. I also need a detonation device so I'll only need to dial one number to activate all three bombs," Joey said.

Looking at Joey while pouring the tea, the young man said, "What you have requested I can provide in four days. The cost is five-thousand dollars. I hope that is not a problem." Joey indicated it was not and that he would bring the money in four days.

Chapter
Sixteen

At 3:15 p.m., Burk tracked down Jeannie who was with Pinheiro and Ismail in the breakroom. "Miranda's gotten some IDs already," Burk said. The three followed him to the large briefing room where Darcy was taping photos onto the large white-board and writing each person's name under their photo.

"Detective Freeman's on his way," said Ismail to no one in particular.

One picture showed Joey identified as Joseph Alan Rogers, 36-years old. He was in uniform and displaying his rank as sergeant. Most of the other photos appeared to have come from Department of Motor Vehicle licensing agencies. Another photo was of Victoria Reynolds, 42--years old. She looked like a 1960's college radical, and yet another was the photo of an obese Mexican-Americas named Armando "Chico" Fernandez, 27 years old. Amy

Nelson was a very pretty girl sporting a large brown hair-do. She could easily pass as a high school student and was the baby of the group at only 18-years old. The unsmiling photo of 25-year old Sandi Marie Osborne showed a young woman who was or had been battling facial acne. Finally, a photo of someone named William "Billy" Wagner rounded out the rows of now identified Pavlenko and his security team's killers. Billy was 24-years old. His photo was from the California Department of Corrections; it was his booking photo.

"We should have a lot of background information to share by tomorrow morning," Darcy said. "Miranda and her team are awesome," she added.

Just then Detective Freeman and his partner arrived. "Hey Freeman, let me introduce you to everyone," Flores said. Upon completing introductions, Lomax entered followed by two new replacement agents carrying disposable coffee carriers, paper cups, sugar and crème. "Thought we might need this," Lomax said. Everyone but Darcy helped themselves to coffee.

"OK," Lomax said. "Let's go around the room and see what we do know so far." Jeannie started by saying, "Joey, aka Joseph Alan Rogers, was allowed entrance into Pavlenko's mansion while Victoria Reynolds, Sandi Osborne, Victoria Reynolds, and Billy Wagner waited in the shadows at the side of the residence. The security files show Joey going upstairs where he finds Pavlenko exercising. Pavlenko goes to his safe, and that's when Joey shoots him in the knee. Joey is seen placing his hand over Pavlenko's mouth, and later Pavlenko writes something on a piece of paper. When he's finished writing, Joey shoots him in the head. We assume he used a suppressor since the security team in the monitoring room didn't respond to the third-floor."

"That makes sense," Freeman said. "The patrol units contacted all of the adjacent neighbors who said they did not hear any gunshots. That means the four killers outside were also using suppressors."

Jeannie continued. "Joey goes to the second-floor and takes out the crew in the monitoring room. He's now home free. The file shows him going to a window facing the street and flashing a light signal to the four outside, telling them it's time to take out the exterior guards. Amy joins the group. He then comes downstairs and opens the front door. They drag the two dead guards in front into the residence and then start cleaning out the property, including Pavlenko's wall safe on the third-floor and the massive gun vault."

"That's how we wrote up our report for the DA. They'll be issuing warrants by this afternoon for five counts of homicide on each of those individuals," Freeman said as he pointed to the white-board. "My chief wants to thank you for wrapping up this high-profile case for us. It'll make us look good in the media. How did you get them identified so quickly?" he asked.

Jeannie looked at Pinheiro who said, "We used DHS resources."

Finding three large 16-inch ceramic indoor planter pots at a discount pottery business, Amy and Joey headed to the warehouse near the waterfront. When they arrived, they saw Billy and Chico carrying out leather chairs from the back of a U-Haul truck into a warehouse that had a large conference room badly in need of repair. The curved walnut desks were already in place when Chico and Billy positioned the companion chairs. Joey carried two of the ceramic pots and Amy carried the third into the warehouse where they placed them in front of the two large desks. In those positions the blast radius would have maximum effect. "We forgot flowers," Amy said. "No, we'll buy some the night the court meets after I pick up the product from my friend," Joey responded. All in all, Joey felt the court setup looked fine for what he had planned for the judges.

Almost on cue, Joey received a call from Judge Silverman inquiring if the new Star Chamber would be functional in three days. Joey confirmed that it would be ready. Silverman asked Joey to follow the court's previous procedures and notify the other members of the Star Chamber regarding day, time, and location. Joey entered the conference room and signaled the other member of the SDL to be quiet as he began calling the magistrates. All of the judges acknowledged the needed information and stated they would be there. In three days, Joey and the remaining members of the Sons and Daughters of Liberty would get their revenge once and for all.

The next day, Lomax assembled everyone back in the briefing room after Darcy and Burk told him they had background information for the team. "OK, here we go," said Burk to Jeannie, Lomax, Pinheiro, and Ismail. Darcy was already up front beside Burk. "Joey's full name is Joseph Alan Rogers, a former sergeant with Delta Force. He has a clean DD214 after serving six years in the Army. We didn't find too much about his activities after leaving the military, but down the road he hooked up with William Wagner, known to his friends as Billy. The two were arrested in Newport Beach after they successfully robbed a bank. We're still waiting for complete reports from the Newport PD and our office down there. They were both found guilty and served four years of an eight-year sentence. By the way, we have no current address for either of them."

Darcy jumped in, "We think we may have the motivation that attracted Joey to the Star Chamber. Miranda secured his juvenile records. As a juvenile he was technically never arrested but spent a considerable amount of time in foster care. His father was an alcoholic and abused Joey's mother routinely. When Joey was seven years old, his father severely injured his mother, requiring hospitalization. His father was arrested, and since there was no one to care for Joey, he was placed in child protective service. His mom got a restraining order, but every time she called the police, they talked her out of prosecuting, telling her it was a waste of time. His mother returned to Joey's dad who promised to seek counseling and give up booze. We have all heard the story, right?" she asked, not expecting a reply. "Two years later, his father came home in a drunken rage and this time strangled Joey's mother, killing her in front of Joey. Joey called the emergency line and his father, in panic, fled the scene only to wrap his truck around a telephone pole, dying instantly."

"Jesus," said Ismail. "At seven years old?"

Darcy continued. "He spent time with several different foster parents but couldn't bond with any of them until he was placed in the home of Mr. and Mrs. Gillingham who lost their only son in Viet Nam, a former Green Beret. Mr. Gillingham had also served in the military and ran the household similarly. That seemed to be a good fit for Joey and eventually led him to enlist in the Army."

"Makes sense," said Lomax. "As a kid he sees his dad beat the hell out of his mom, but when the cops arrive, his father is above the law and nothing happens until it's too late."

Darcy moved on to the next photo on the whiteboard. "Armando Fernandez has several driving citations, mostly speed, and nothing major. He ran with the Hells Angels but was never sponsored by the gang, so he moved on. His nickname is Chico and he comes from a large Mexican family. His parents are illegals coming to the U.S. over thirty years ago, so being born in the states, he's a citizen. He's held jobs, mostly working warehouse jobs like Home Depot, Lowes, and auto body painting.

Amy Nelson is the youngest member of the SDL. She was a habitual runaway and in and out of juvenile hall in Oakland. Drugs, alcohol use, and generally acting out. While living on the street she sold her body for money or scrounged dumpsters for food. How she became associated with the SDL, we don't know yet." With that, Burk looked at Darcy who took over.

"Sandi Osborne, spelled on her birth certificate with an i instead of a y, and Victoria Reynold, called Vicki, have arrest convictions stemming from campus uprisings at the University of California, Berkeley as well as other colleges. She met Vicki while in college, and friends indicate they're lovers. Most of their charges were for vandalism, assault, and public urination, peeing on signs that announce events they oppose. On one occasion however, the two hooked up with a professor and tried to blackmail him. They were both arrested, but the DA dropped the charge when the professor changed his mind about pressing charges. It appears that Vicki has never held a job nor filed income tax. She was a professional student.

GARY J. ROSE

"Sandi comes from a wealthy family which she rejected. Her parents haven't seen her for years and have no idea where she is. What's still missing is how Joey recruited them to become members of the SDL."

Burk took over. "That brings us to the final member of the SDL, William Wagner, known to his friends as Billy. As we said earlier, Billy and Joey pulled off a daring bank robbery in Southern California, specifically Newport Beach. According to the police report we obtained late yesterday, they had planned the heist for two weeks. They would have escaped, except their getaway car, get this, ran out of gas while the police were in pursuit. They tried to escape on foot. Can't hide very well from a copter, and they were both caught."

"Like they say, we only catch the dumb ones," Ismail said.

Burk said they were both found guilty and served four years of an eight-year sentence and concluded with, "By the way, we have no current addresses for any of the SDL members yet."

"We do have addresses on known associates, relatives and so forth, and our collogues including the SFPD are tracking them down," Jeannie said to the assembled group. "But for right now, we're chasing paper trails."

Chapter Seventeen

Joey placed a bomb on the bottom of each of the two ceramic planter pots. Amy followed, placing fresh flowers they bought at a local grocery store on top to hide what lie below. Joey stood back, placing himself dead center in front of the two curved desks and admired the staging and flowers. *Freshly cut flowers for their funerals*, he thought as he glanced at his watch. He made sure there was power coming from the generator behind the warehouse for the laptop the justices would use to present their cases. Everything was set. He told the girls they could take the van and return to their safe house, giving them money to pick up food. *Blowing assholes up makes a person hungry*, he thought, catching a smile on his face. Billy and Chico would be parked several blocks away in their second car and would pick up Joey after they heard the explosion.

First to arrive was Judge Roberts. He nodded at Joey who escorted him into the Star Chamber. Roberts donned his black robe and checked out the conference room. Judges Kavanaugh and Kalford arrived within minutes of each other. Seeing Kavanaugh enter the side of the warehouse, Kalford followed his path. Judges Hall, Silverman and Henderson arrived at three-minute intervals. Joey re-entered the Star Chamber, finding all judges dressed much like Judge Roberts. Small talk took place between the Judges until Judge Silverman hit the oak block on the desk with the gavel. *I guess the judges decided Silverman would be the first presiding judge of the new Star Chamber*, Joey thought. Joey lowered the lights and turned on the laptop showing a female member of the House of Representatives. Someone booed, but then decorum took over. Joey slid out of the entrance and locked the door behind him.

Using a flashlight, he walked a block and a half away and surveyed the surrounding area. Seeing no one, he proceeded to pull out the cell phone connected wirelessly to the two bombs. Looking back in the direction of the warehouse, he placed his right index finger over the call button, but before hitting the key, he said the names of the deceased members of the SDL who were killed on the orders of those justices now in the warehouse.

The blast lite up the sky as if daylight had quickly replaced the night. A brilliant yellow fireball traveled forty-feet in the air that Chico and Billy saw from their vantage point. Chico started up the car and drove to the pre-arranged location where they found Joey. Joey's ears where deaf from the blast, but he was able to say with a smile while entering the van, "The Star Chamber will not be in session again." There was no doubt in his mind that everyone inside the warehouse had perished.

As they drove out of the warehouse district, they could hear sirens responding. No doubt the sound of the blast could be heard for miles. Joey wondered how long it would take law enforcement to identify the remains. *Doesn't matter,* he thought. They were moving on to the next target.

Jeannie woke first the next morning with Pinheiro on his side facing away from her. She thought about sliding out of bed and not disturbing him, but changed her mind. She turned to face him and placed her arm around his waist, finally placing it on his chest. She then scooted her waist against his buttocks and quickly fell back asleep. *God, how I love this man,* she thought as she drifted off. Around 9:00 a.m., Jeannie's phone vibrated on the nightstand. She looked at the display and saw that it was Tami, her secretary. "Hi Tami, what's up?" Jeannie asked. "What? Where? When did that happen?" she said into the phone as she sat up. The conversation awakened Ricky who turned on to his side facing Jeannie. "OK. Get hold of Ismail and have him meet me there. We'll be driving up Highway 880. My ETA is in about one hour."

She turned to Ricky and told him what Tami had relayed. An abandoned warehouse on the west side of Oakland near the waterfront blew up the night before. Oakland PD found six bodies inside, but burned beyond recognition. "It has to be the Star Chamber. They started back up," she said.

"I'm happy to say our comrades didn't die in vain. The Star Chamber is no more," Joey boasted to the group. Vicki started to clap with Sandi following her lead. "Now that we have that behind us, we can discuss our plans to kidnap Mr. Sadler's teenage daughter. Vicki, what did you and Sandi learn from your scouting expedition yesterday?" he asked.

Chapter Eighteen

J oey was the first to enter the kitchen. Everyone else was still asleep after a long night of partying over the end of the Star Chamber. He decided to take a quick run to the corner liquor store and buy a newspaper so he could read how the fake media described the event. He wasn't disappointed; it was the lead item on the front page.

"Six People Killed in Warehouse Explosion"

The article did not state any connection to the Star Chamber. It simply stated that an explosion had occurred in an abandoned warehouse in West Oakland and that to date six bodies had been found. The dead were not identified, and the paper said it would not publish names until relatives were notified. Joey knew the police would have to rely on dental records and DNA to identify the dead judges, but he didn't care. He got his revenge.

Returning home, Joey found Amy still in her panties and white t-shirt eating a bowl of Coco puffs at the kitchen table. Joey showed her the newspaper and she smiled. "How was your run?" she asked.

"Great, the air is so clean in the early morning hours. After breakfast, you and I need to take a ride down to Atherton in San Mateo county," he said.

"Is that where Sadler's house is?" Amy asked.

"Yeah. I just want to check it out," Joey said as he filled a bowel with cereal and milk.

Ricky was already creating a breakfast delight in the kitchen when Jeannie walked in wearing the sexy satin and lace chemise from the previous night. "Smells good," she said, as Ricky handed her a hot cup of coffee. "Are you going to continue to make breakfast for me after we get married?" she asked after taking her first sip.

"You keep dressing like that in the morning and you can count on breakfast every day," he said leering at her with the hint of a smile.

He plated two plates on the countertop and took them over to the kitchen table. The two talked about their childhoods, their likes and dislikes about movies, sports, and cars. They shared the same political points of view and Ricky told her that a purge of the holdover appointees of Obama were also being removed, similar to those in the FBI. Ricky picked up the empty plates, and after rinsing them, put them in the dishwasher.

Jeannie brought over the two coffee cups and was preparing to refill them when Ricky took them from her hands and placed them on the counter near the Cuisinart coffee maker. He then turned into Jeannie and started kissing her while caressing her breasts. His hands lowered the shoulder straps dropping the chemise onto the kitchen floor. Jeannie responded by pulling the t-shirt Ricky wore over his head dropping it onto her chemise. She then grabbed the front of his sweatpants and pulled them down to his feet. He quickly pulled his feet free of the cotton pants and their sexual exploration went into overdrive.

Fifteen minutes later, both still lying on the kitchen floor, Jeannie said, "If your cousin saw us now, he would say something like, who's the perverts now?" Ricky started to laugh and then Jeannie said, "Oh my God," jumping up and quickly putting on her nightgown. "What if Delores was looking in the kitchen window?"

Ricky started to laugh even louder while getting up, grabbing his sweatpants and t-shirt. "Well, if she did, she probably ran right home and is now giving Mr. Delores the time of his life," he said. Jeannie ran into his waiting arms and laughed almost as loud as he was. "God, we are bad," Jeannie said into Ricky's chest.

"Actually, I thought it was damn good," he replied.

The sign on the side of the van read AAA plumbing. "What's with the sign?" Amy asked Joey as they walked toward the vehicle. Joey was carrying a toolbox and opened the side sliding door, placing it on the floor. He then closed the door and looked at the magnetic sign.

"People don't notice repairmen. They remember the color of their uniform and the color of the vehicle, but that's it. The uniform can get you into almost anywhere."

They drove south down Highway 101 to Atherton, a very wealthy neighborhood attracting sport figures, celebrities, and politicians--people like Howard Sadler. Joey told Amy that Atherton was ranked as having the highest per capita income among U.S. towns with a population between 2,500 and 9,999. "Looks like it. Gee, these homes and yards are huge," she said.

"Yeah," Joey continued, "It's regularly ranked as the most expensive ZIP Code in the United States. At one time Ty Cobb, the Hall of Fame Major League Baseball player, lived here. I'm not sure if NBA star for the Golden State Stephen Curry, or Hall of Famer Willie Mays, or, 49ers wide receiver Jerry Rice still live there or not, but a lot of upper-crust people call it home."

They found Salder's estate, and like all the other properties, it was huge. The entire estate was completely enclosed by an eight-foot wrought iron fence, the front gate monitored by cameras and a call box. Joey and Amy counted three gorgeous German Shepherds running around the manicured lawn as well as two uniformed, but unarmed, security officers sitting near the oversized entrance doors to the main structure.

The residence was four-stories tall. Without an architectural drawing, Joey could only guess the layout, which was not good for someone thinking about storming the house. They drove around the neighborhood and saw that adjacent homes also had more than adequate security. Joey decided that the estate was too hardened a target to attempt the kidnapping there. He had to come up with a different plan. They drove through a Chic-fil-A and got two chicken sandwiches and sodas and parked in a grocery store parking lot to eat. "What should we do?" asked Amy while wiping her face with a napkin.

"You and I can't keep driving around the neighborhood in the van. People will start to question why we're there. No, instead, I'll have Vicki and Sandi take our other car and watch activity at the house for the next few days. They can drive around or park and stroll hand in hand. The people who live in this liberal neighborhood wouldn't question two lesbians making out on the sidewalk. Let's get home."

Jeannie showered first and decided to let her hair air dry. When Ricky came out of the bathroom he called for Jeannie. "In here," she said, looking at her spare bedroom wall.

Ricky entered and said, "When did you do this?" On the wall were duplicate pictures of the SDL with Joey's picture in the center and strings going to various other pictures. "Last night after we made love. I couldn't sleep, so got up quietly and came in here."

"Did you get anything out of it?" Ricky asked as he stepped forward and looked at Jeannie's work.

"Not really, but I did come up with something we could follow up on until we get a solid lead," she said.

"What's that?" he asked.

"Well, remember when either Burk or Darcy talked about Joey's tragic life? The fact that his father killed his mother…"

Ricky replied, "Yeah, so?"

"Well, here's what I'm thinking. Mother's Day is almost here. Somewhere I read where his mother is buried."

"OK, now I know where this is going?" Ricky said. "What the hell, I don't think you have anything else to work on. Maybe we'll luck out."

Chapter Nineteen

Jeannie missed waking up next to Ricky, but duty called and he had to return to D.C., but would return in two weeks. That Saturday she received verification that her request for three surveillance teams would be in place the next morning, Mother's Day. She agreed with Ricky that it was a long shot, but so far none of her agents assigned to the investigation had turned up anything. Relatives, friends, associates had nothing to offer in their search for the killers. Bomb experts did verify that it was two homemade bombs detonated remotely that killed the six people in the warehouse explosion. DNA matches identified the six magistrates. Jeannie was sure they had decided the heat was off and it was safe to start up the Star Chamber again. She had also put two and two together and believed that Joey was the mastermind who convinced the six judges to attend the abandoned warehouse where they would meet their end. All out of revenge for the three fallen former SDL members ordered killed by the court.

Her thoughts turned to her deceased mother with Mother's Day almost upon her. Her mother had passed away several years earlier, but she always placed flowers on her grave on special occasions such as her birthday and Christmas. Fortunately, she was in a different cemetery than the one being staked out. She would get up early, miss Ricky's famous breakfast, and after grabbing something to eat, pick up some flowers and head to the resting spot. From there she would head in the general direction of the stakeout, but well out of the immediate area.

Joey and the SDL were gathered in the small front room of their safe house. Once again, he had a large piece of cardboard showing several drawings. "Based on the great work by Vicki and Sandi, I think we now have a great idea on how to proceed with the kidnapping of Sadler's daughter. Sadler's house has too much security. Charlotte Sadler attends this private high school. Each school day, she's driven by a chauffeur to and from, taking the same route each day. As you can see, the limo has to stop at this intersection to make a left-hand turn. Next Monday, Billy and Amy, you will drive the Ford Focus here— pointing to the drawing—and make it look like you're having car trouble. When the chauffeur stops for the stop sign, he'll see that you are blocking his left turn.

I'll drive up behind the limo with Vicki and Sandi. Billy will come up to the driver's door and ask if he can make a call for a tow. Once the driver puts the car in park, Billy will put one in his head.

"Quickly, Vicki and Sandi will jump out of the van, leaving the door open. You two will run up to the right passenger side of the limo, and after opening the door, you'll grab Charlotte from the back seat. You must do it fast enough so she can't use her cellphone. If she's already on the phone, slap it out of her hands before she can say anything about what's happening. I'll drive up next to the limo in the van. You two will push Charlotte into the van and follow her inside. Billy will return to the Focus. Each vehicle will take a different route back to the safe house. Any questions?

Jeannie and Ismael were parked outside of the cemetery, but close enough that they could see Joey's mother's grave without binoculars. About 30 feet away, recently transferred agents Alicia Anthony and Steven Wilcock's had spread a blanket on the grass near a grave and were rearranging flowers they had placed on the headstone. On a knoll in the opposite direction, Agent Davenport sat on a donated concrete bench reading a book. A half-block away, Agents Brooke Adams and her partner Scott Larson were seated in a Chevrolet Impala in case the suspect or suspects tried to flee the scene. As hours passed without any sign of Joey or SDL members, Jeannie began moving the teams around to keep the charade changing. By late afternoon Jeannie knew her hunch was not going to pay off and canceled the surveillance teams. She and Ismail started their car and headed back to the bureau. From their vantage point they could not see a male watching all of the FBI activity in his binoculars. "Sorry Mom," Joey said aloud to himself in the Focus. "I'll bring flowers as soon as I can. I love you."

Howard Sadler was a multi-billionaire. With the large amount of seed money he inherited from his parents, he developed one of the largest firms that supplied parts for major smartphones. The parts were manufactured on the sweat of third-world employees making $2.00 a day, working 14-hours, Monday through Saturday. He and his wife belonged to three country clubs, owned a superyacht, and both drove matching Jaguars. Charlotte, their only child, just turned 17-years old and was a stuck-up bitch having been born with a silver spoon in her mouth. She never desired a driver's license. She didn't need one with a limo at her beckon call.

Monica Stromberg married Howard when she was 20-years old; not for love, but for his money which, as his company grew, she could spend lavishly. She was five inches taller than her husband, which wasn't saying much since he only stood 5'3". But what he lacked in height, he made up for in weight: 320 pounds. Always sporting a tan, sometimes sprayed on, she loved spending time playing tennis at one of the country clubs in the area. She sponsored galas at their estate and never found a cause that she and Howard did not donate too, especially if it generated a lot of media coverage or future political favoritism.

Charlotte was an inconvenience. Discovering her pregnancy too late, she chose to go ahead with the birth to avoid scandal if it leaked out she had had an abortion. Charlotte began attending private pre-schools, ballet, gymnastics, anything that would put her in the spotlight next to Monica. Monica controlled with whom Charlotte developed friends and was currently scouting what she considered the best university for her daughter to attend upon her upcoming graduation.

Howard could care less. Trapped in a loveless marriage, he traveled often and paid for the services of expensive call girls whenever he had the need. At one time he had a mistress, but she became too demanding, so he terminated the relationship and gave her some quiet money. *No*, he thought. *Screwing call girls was the way to go. No attachment issues. Just pure sex.* Sure, there was the risk of STDs, but he dismissed the worry by having several doctors on standby who would be paid for their discretion.

His doctors had recently told him that his blood pressure was extremely high, no doubt related to his obesity. They recommended that he take drastic action and undergo a gastric bypass. Further consideration for the surgery came when a newspaper showed a picture of him wearing a tuxedo, commenting that he looked and walked like a fat penguin. His agent had already scheduled him for a flight to Cancun where the surgery would be performed in private. He would stay there for at least a month, supposedly taking a well-deserved vacation.

On Monday morning, everything was set. Driving the van with the magnetic plumbing sign, Joey followed the chauffeured-limo from the Sadler estate along its regular route to school. Sandi and Vicki were in the back of the van with Vicki holding the side door handle so they could quickly exit the vehicle when the time arrived.

The driver approached the stop sign and saw the Ford Focus blocking his left-turn with its hood up. Billy began walking purposefully back to the limo. The chauffeur rolled down the window and asked what the problem was. Billy told them the car just died and asked if the driver could call a tow. Putting the limo in park, the chauffeur reached for the phone, but before he reached it, Billy fired two shots from his semi-automatic with an attached suppressor into the left side of his head. Even with the suppressor, the sound of the weapon firing not once but twice caused Charlotte to scream from the back seat. She had a cellphone in her right hand and had been texting when the passenger door quickly opened. Vicki quickly reached in and slapped it out of her hand.

Grabbing Charlotte's long auburn hair, she pulled the teenager from the backseat into the waiting arms of Sandi who placed a pillowcase over her head. Vicki and Sandi then forcibly lead her to the opened side door of the van and threw her inside, then climbed in and slammed the door shut. Her cellphone laid on the floor of the limo still receiving unanswered text messages.

Jeannie had set her alarm for 6 a.m. so she could get a light workout in before heading across the bay. But, when it went off, she hit the snooze button, rolled over onto the pillow used by Ricky, and picking up his scent went back to sleep. The vibration of her cell phone soon interrupted her slumber. It was the office. "Good morning, Tami," she said.

"Sorry for waking you up, Jeannie, but the SAC has called for an all hands-on-deck meeting in two hours.

"What's up?" Jeannie asked.

"A little over an hour ago, Howard Sadler's teenage daughter, Charlotte was kidnapped, and her limo driver was killed," Tami reported.

Chapter Twenty

J eannie got off the elevator and stopped at Tami's desk. "Any new developments?" she asked.

"Not to my knowledge," was the reply.

"Hey, boss, did you get to the gym?" asked Ismail handing her a cup of coffee.

"No. I'd hoped to sleep in, but here I am," Jeannie said. "So, what do we know?" she asked as the two headed toward her office.

"Kid was being driven to her private school in a limo. Looks like the perps had an ambush set up since as soon as the limo driver stopped, he took two in the head. Sadler's seventeen-year-old daughter Charlotte was taken from the backseat and is gone. Her cellphone was on the floor near where she was seated. It took some planning."

"Witnesses, video, anything?" Jeannie asked.

"Not so far," Ismail said. "The Sadler's live in Atherton, and you know how the high-brows out there feel about having cameras at intersections. It's an invasion of their privacy. If the Sadler's were part of that group, I'll bet they wish they'd requested video camera installations, because right now, we've got nothing to go on. There are approximately seven-thousand people living there, and residences are so spread out due to each parcel's size, it's almost rural. The Atherton PD has already formally requested our help and the SAC wants everyone, and I mean everyone, in the briefing room in thirty-five minutes.

Making sure no one was watching; Vicki and Sandi pulled the hooded Charlotte from the side van door and took her into the safe house kitchen, then walked her down the narrow hallway to a hall closet and pushed her inside leaving the pillowcase on. "If you open the door bitch, you're dead," said Vicki.

Soon everyone had returned from the kidnapping site, and keeping an eye on the hall closet door, they met in the front room. "Good job everyone," Joey said. "Everyone performed with military precision. Now we let time work for us." Glancing at his watch, Joey told the group that by now the cops had already been notified and they would be requesting FBI aid. Sadler's residence phones would be monitored, expecting a ransom call.

"Is that what we're going to do?" asked Amy.

"Not yet," Joey answered. I want frustration to set in with the Sadler's as well as law enforcement.

We'll wait four to five days and then send them a communique. I bet Vicki, our academia specialist, knows what I'm shooting for. Right Vicki?"

Vicki loved being referred to as the most intelligent member of the group. "Sure do," she said. Looking at the group, she asked if anyone remembered the Symbionese Liberation Army (SLA) and the kidnapping of Patty Hearst. She was not surprised that no one except Joey knew anything, so she gave them a brief history.

"The Symbionese Liberation Army was an American left-wing terrorist organization active between 1973 and 1975. The group committed bank robberies, two murders and other acts of violence. The SLA became internationally notorious for the kidnapping of heiress Patricia Hearst, abducting the nineteen-year-old from Berkeley, California. She later joined the SLA. I believe Joey's plan is for us to duplicate that famous case with Charlotte Sadler as our Patty Hearst."

"You should've been a professor, Vicki. You did an excellent job outlining our little plan with Ms. Sadler back there," Joey said to the delight of Vicki. "I want you and Sandi to do some research on the whole SLA kidnapping event and construct a note we'll send not only to the Sadler's, but also selected media outlets. Pick up some of the dialogue the SLA used during their time of reign. Take your time since it's on our side for now," said Joey. "For the rest of us, it's time for rest and relaxation. With the Star Chamber and now our first kidnapping, I think we're due some time off. Amy, put a bucket in the closet for Charlotte so she can go to the bathroom as needed. Turn on the light and remove her pillow case. Her indoctrination will start this evening."

During the briefing, the SAC admitted that no evidence had emerged from the crime scene. "An autopsy is scheduled for later this afternoon and maybe the slugs might give them something to work on. The limo driver was shot from approximately two feet away, so the shooter was able to get up close. The victim was texting her girlfriend whom we've tracked down. She couldn't offer much more than what was on the texts themselves except for Charlotte's screams. Jeannie, I want you and Ismael to contact the Sadler's at their residence. Right now, all we can do is follow the bureau's playbook for a ransom kidnapping. Make sure the two of you are back here by four p.m. for a press conference. OK, let's go people. The clock's ticking," he said as he left the room.

Jeannie and Ismail headed south on Highway 101 to Atherton. "Did you know that Atherton is ranked as having the highest per-capita income among U.S. towns?" Ismail asked.

"Gee, aren't you a wealth of information this morning. Pardon the pun about wealth," Jeannie said.

"Yeah, if you like that, here's some more. The median income for a household in the town is in excess of nine-hundred and fifty thousand, the highest of any place in the United States," he said with a smile as he concentrated on weaving in and out of slow traffic. "And I'll bet you still can't find a house at that price."

Once they were close to the Sadler estate, it wasn't hard to find the location since they counted at least eleven media trucks and vans, most with their satellite antennas already up. "Must be the place?" Ismail said as he flashed his credentials to the uniformed officer at the front gate, who called someone on his radio. Shortly, the large entrance gate opened.

"God, look at this place. It looks like a park," Jeannie remarked.

"Yeah, a park the size of a golf course," replied Ismail.

"How much is this guy worth?" Jeannie asked.

"Around three and a half-billion," Ismail said.

"Well shit, he can afford it I guess," Jeannie replied.

Several law enforcement cars were parked near the front entrance. "Shit!" said Jeannie. I'll bet we're going to be boxed in when it's time to leave." They found another uniformed office at the front door and both Jeannie and Ismael showed him their identification. He opened the door and they followed the sound of conversation emanating from the large grand room overlooking a huge swimming pool and tennis court. Two FBI agents were setting up monitoring and recording equipment on a table and they both nodded at Ismail and Jeannie when they entered. Sitting on a leather couch, but not next to each other, was Howard Sadler and his wife.

Monica Sadler looked as if she had just come from a beauty salon, her hair recently coiffured in a French Bob style with highlights. She had tears in her eyes and massacre streaks on her cheeks which she dabbed with an embroidered handkerchief with the letters M.S. A picture of Charlotte dressed in her private school uniform was on the table. *Bet she liked wearing that*, Jeannie thought.

Jeannie could not think of another couple who seemed to be more opposite of one another than the Sadler's. Monica was prime and proper, and appeared to have had a boob-job in the past as well as several facelifts. Her nails would never had allowed her to type on a computer. Furthermore, Jeannie doubted her eyelashes were natural. The jewelry around her neck was probably worth more than the yearly salary of her and Ismail combined. Howard was wearing black slacks and a black and white designer pullover sweater, looking like an orca sitting on the side of a trainer's ledge waiting to be rewarded with a sardine for a recently completed trick. His combover looked atrocious and his glasses made him look like a Celestial eye goldfish, or Groucho Marx trying to blow up a balloon.

After introducing herself and Ismail, Jeannie asked the Sadler's to relate the day's events before the incident occurred. Howard looked at his wife as if to ask permission to speak. Monica leaned forward holding her handkerchief and began. "Charlotte is always awakened by Stephanie, our maid. She leaves Charlotte to get ready and notifies the kitchen help that they should start her breakfast. Stephanie said that Charlotte came downstairs already dressed for school and ate her breakfast, then grabbed her books and went out the door where Manny, our chauffer, was waiting to drive her to school. Oh, my poor daughter, where have they taken you," she said dabbing her eyes again, but in a way to make sure her remaining makeup stayed impeccable. "Everyone loves Charlotte. No one would want to harm her."

"So, you didn't see your daughter this morning?" Ismail asked.

"Oh no. She has to leave so early for school, I was still asleep. Howard and I have tried numerous times to have the school change their ungodly instruction hours, right Howard?"

Howard seemed startled at being asked to participate in the conversation going on in front of him. "Yes, yes. We've had several meetings with the school's administration, but to no avail," he said, looking at his wife to see if he did a good enough job. Howard also stated that he was in his study making phone calls and did not see his daughter off.

In addition to Stephanie, Jeannie and Ismail interviewed the remaining house staff, but learned nothing useful. No one had seen any strangers or vehicles in the previous days. They checked with the phone monitoring team and told them to advise them if any calls were received. Jeannie and Ismail left the Sadler's sitting on their leather couch, and began their drive back to the bureau.

Chapter
Twenty-one

"Charlotte, Charlotte," Joey said, knocking on the closed closet door. Then, he shouted, "Charlotte!" while banging on the door. He could hear sobbing coming from inside the tiny room. "I want to go home," Charlotte cried. "Please, let me go home."

"Home. Why do you want to go home? Your parents don't want you. They don't love you. You're just a leech that uses money they earn off the backs of third-country workers who toil away, putting parts together for your father's company for two dollars a day. Two dollars a day, while your fat fuck of a father sits on his ass counting the money he makes selling these parts to cellphone manufacturers at an exorbitant amount. You do know what exorbitant means don't you Charlotte." There was no response from the closet. Then the crying started again. "Hush, hush sweet Charlotte. Charlotte don't you cry," sang

Joey into the door, followed by more heavy banging. *That was a great movie. Scared the crap out of me when I first saw the flick. Bette Davis was a great actress,* he thought.

Joey told Amy to take the car and pick up food for the group as well as Charlotte. Vicki and Sandi were in the kitchen working on the notes they would deliver to the Atherton PD and several media outlets. Joey then talked to Chico and Billy alone outside. "You'll be the first tonight," Joey told Billy. "Tomorrow night, she'll be yours, Chico."

The press spokeswoman, an FBI agent herself, tapped on the microphone attached to the podium. "OK, if everyone can take a seat, we'd like to get started," she said. "My name is Special Agent Nancy Hoffman and I want to set some ground rules before I introduce Special Agent in Charge Lomax and Assistant Special Agent in Charge Loomis. Because this is an active investigation, we'll only discuss previous events of the day, nothing specific about the investigation process itself. I hope everyone is clear on that." She scanned the room and no one seemed to object. "Very well, SAC Lomax," she said yielding the podium.

"This morning at approximately seven forty-five, seventeen-year-old Charlotte Sadler was abducted on her way to school while driven by a chauffeur in her father's company limousine. At this intersection here--pointing to a picture on the wall showing street names--the limousine stopped for some reason and the driver was shot and killed. Charlotte was taken from the backseat and apparently taken to a waiting vehicle in the area. The Atherton Police Department requested FBI assistance which has now taken over jurisdiction." Lomax looked at Jeannie and stepped away from the podium.

"Hello bitch," Joey said, who with the rest of the SDL was watching a used television set in the front room. He continued, "Everyone, this is Special Agent Jeannie Loomis, the one who was always a step behind us while we carried out sentences for the Star Chamber. I was actually in her house once. The court wanted me to see if she kept her investigation records at home. I tell you, she has a nosy neighbor that's hard to avoid. She didn't have anything in her house, so we assumed her material was kept at work. That's why I ordered a raid on her office in Roseville to get their records and Judge Baldwin's laptop. So, you're chasing us again, Agent Loomis? Bring it on!"

"Hi," Ricky said when Jeannie answered her phone.
"Hi to you as well. God, I miss you," Jeannie said as she continued her drive across the Dumbarton Bridge.
"I saw you on the news this afternoon. You got a bad one, huh?" he asked.

"Yes, it's bad, "Jeannie answered. "We have nothing to follow up on so far. The suspect or suspects haven't made any ransom demands, and there were no mounted cameras at the intersection to show the abduction. Frankly, we have zip, nada."

"Sorry love. But maybe what I have to tell you might brighten your day. I'm waiting for my flight to San Jose and I can spend two weeks with you.

"Oh my God! That would be great! When does your plane arrive, and why San Jose?" she asked. "Well, I just got permission for the days off, and thought I'd either fly out tomorrow and have you pick me up at SFO, or take an earlier flight, putting me in San Jose after you get off work. I didn't want you to have to drive back to the city. My flight arrives at ten forty-five p.m. I hope that's alright," he said.

"More than alright! I'll be in the cellphone lot by 10:30, so text me when you're in the arrival area.

"Hello Charlotte," Billy said as he opened the closet door. It's time for you to take a hot bath. You must be getting ripe in here. I'm sorry, but I have to put this pillowcase back over your head. Stand up," he ordered. She had a hard time maintaining her balance at first, but then steadied herself and started to sob as Billy covered her head. "Grab my hand and follow me," he said. She complied, and for the first time in almost sixteen hours, she was able to leave the closet and walk. She knew she had reached the bathroom when she heard water splashing into the tub, and that was confirmed when Billy closed the bathroom door and took off the pillowcase. The tub had about four inches of water already, so Billy shut the water off. "OK, it's all yours," he said.

Charlotte stood shaking, looking down at the worn linoleum floor. "What, you want me to take off your clothes?" Billy asked with a lustful smile on his face. Charlotte did not reply as the tears ran down her face. Shouting, Billy said, "Take off your clothes bitch!" Charlotte jumped at the command and began unbuttoning the white school uniform blouse. "Nice tits," he said looking at her white bra. She then unzipped her blue skirt and let it fall to the floor, turning her back to Billy and unsnapped her bra, catching it and placing it on the toilet. Without changing position, she pulled down her underpants. "Turn around," Billy said. Charlotte did as she was told, placing one arm in front of her breasts and the other over her vagina. "Get in," Billy said. Charlotte grabbed the side of the tub with the hand she had used to conceal her breasts and climbed in, and then placed it over her breasts. "Shy, huh?" Billy asked. "Don't worry, I will grow on you."

Ricky's flight was delayed forty-minutes, but Jeannie didn't mind. She sat in her Corvette listening to *Hitting Rock Bottom*, her latest audiobook. She caught herself smiling and choking up, hearing the true stories of at-risk students explain their dysfunctional family lives and how, through attending a military-style academy, they turned their lives around. *Order, structure, and discipline for some kids is the right recipe for success*, she thought. Finally, she received Ricky's text and headed to the pickup spot. There he was: the love of her life.

"Hello, Agent Loomis," he crooned.

"Hello, Agent Pinheiro," Jeanne replied. "Would you like a ride to Newark? There's an excellent bed-and-breakfast there."

"It's not the one where the next-door neighbor sneaks around looking into perverts' homes it is?" They kissed and headed for Jeannie's home. On the way they stopped and picked up a pizza. Ricky said the food on the plane left a lot to be desired.

Charlotte climbed out of the tub and waited for Billy, who staring at her body, to hand her a towel. "I have to use the restroom," she said. Billy stepped aside and said, "go ahead." Charlotte sat on the toilet, and after finishing peeing, wiped herself and stood up, reaching for her clothes. "You can put them on later," Billy said, as he put the pillowcase back on her head and led her back to the closet. Before putting her inside he removed the head covering, allowing Charlotte to see that there were five other people staring at her nakedness. She began to cry uncontrollably and freely entered the closet with Billy closing the door.

Ricky entered the front room and placed his small suitcase on the floor near the couch. Famished, he quickly served Jeannie and himself a few slices of pizza and a beer. Going for his third slice, he asked if there had been any contact between the hostage-takers and the family since he last talked before boarding his plane. Jeannie said nothing had changed. Her agents and the Atherton PD had interviewed up to 75 people--friends, relatives, and neighbors--and they still had no leads. "Do you think it's for ransom, or could it be something else?" he asked.

"Come with me, Ace, and tell me what you think," she said, grabbing his hand and leading him upstairs. On the way, he grabbed his suitcase.

Entering the spare room, Ricky saw a photograph of Charlotte Sadler on the wall-mounted whiteboard along with photos of her mother, father, the limo driver, and most of the domestic staff. Under her father Howard's photo, Jeannie had written his worth: three to four-billion dollars. There was also a handwritten note stating that the Sadler's had a living trust as well as a ten-million dollar life insurance policy on each other. Ricky examined the display and asked Jeannie about Charlotte. "Does she have a life insurance policy?" he asked.

"No," Jeannie answered. "We checked."

"What are the possibilities that Charlotte's behind the whole kidnapping? You know, she asks for a high ransom. Her parents pay, and then after she gets the money she flees with an unknown boyfriend."

"I ran that possibility through the Behavioral Analysis Unit in Quantico and they said that it was highly unlikely, but there's always that chance. I don't see it myself. Charlotte's so accustomed to playing her father and mother against each other to get what she wants, why would she blow a good thing. But, as you suggest, if she's hooked up with a low-life, who knows. We went through her social media accounts, cellphone records, you name it, and there's no boyfriend that we can see nor any red flags."

"You know, sometimes a boyfriend can get you to do something you normally wouldn't consider," Ricky said, as he pressed his chest against Jeannie's back and reached around, putting his hands on her breasts.

"And sometimes, a fiancée can get her boyfriend to do something he might not even envision," Jeannie said as she pressed her buttocks into Ricky's groin.

Chapter
Twenty-two

A t 10:45 p.m., Joey told the group to gather around the closed closet door and take a seat on the floor. He looked at Billy who was standing and told him it was time. Billy quickly opened the door, startling Charlotte who had fallen asleep after to the shock of the day.

"Get up!" Billy shouted. The still nude Charlotte did as she was told, still trying to conceal her private areas. "Put your hands down at your side, now!" he shouted. Charlotte began to cry and started to shake. Billy threw a blanket on the floor behind her and said, "Lie down." Charlotte reached for the blanket, thinking she had something to cover herself. "No bitch, leave it on the floor and lay down." Charlotte began to lie sideway on the blanket, facing away from Billy and the onlookers until Billy grabbed her legs and quickly turned her over face up. Charlotte began to scream realizing what was about to happen. Billy slapped her so hard her lip began to bleed and swell. Billy began taking off his clothes with Vicki saying, "Give it to her." This caused the rest of the group to begin chanting, "Go, go, go."

There was no foreplay, just animalistic lust on Billy's part. Charlotte screamed and tried to resist, but repeated slaps by Billy caused her to give into the inevitable. Billy stood after he climaxed and found blood on his penis. "Damn, she was a virgin," he said. "Lucky me." He then slammed the closet door after throwing Charlotte's clothes inside.

Ricky did a few things around Jeannie's house while she was at the bureau, keeping a constant lookout for Delores. He had Jeannie bring home paint and supplies, and he had already painted the downstairs and kitchen while listening to Fox News on the television set where the kidnapping of Charlotte Sadler was the main topic. He was preparing to paint the upstairs and felt he had enough time to complete it before he had to return to Washington. Jeannie loved to come home and find a homemade dinner waiting for her, but she noticed her clothes getting a little tight recently and knew she needed to hit the gym. The only exercise she had been getting lately was with Ricky, and not the type of exercise she would get at her gym.

"Three days have passed and I think it's now time to shake up the FBI," Joey said to the SDL. "Vicki and Sandi made an excellent first communique for the media and law enforcement. Looks very similar to those used by the Symbionese Liberation Army. You two ladies have resurrected them from the dead." Looking at the two, he said, "Take the car, drive over to Oakland and use the mailbox that's on the corner. You know which one I mean. There are no video cameras there, so they'll not be able to determine who put the envelopes in the box. When you return, I'll make a phone call to the number the FBI's been placing on the television and hint that a ransom demand is about to be made. Before I forget, Vicki, you and Sandi need to have Charlotte place her fingerprints on the letter inside each envelope. OK, off you go."

As soon as Vicki and Sandi left, Joey went into the bedroom he shared with Amy and came back with an old portable tape recorder that he placed on the table and inserted a tape. "Boy, that's old school," said Chico.

"Yeah, but very efficient. If we make sure there're no prints or transfer DNA, the FBI will only be able to listen, gaining no evidence beyond the tape," said Joey. Sandi handed him a piece of paper containing what Vicki felt would be an appropriate first communication with the police. Joey looked at it and asked for clarification on a few items, but made no revisions.

With the ransom letters about ready to be mailed, he felt it was time to ratchet up the game. He entered the small master bathroom alone and shut the door, wanting to make sure no background noise could be picked up that the FBI could use to track their location, which he felt was very unlikely. He turned the tape recorder on and began to read from the paper. "This is the leader of the SDL, the Sons and Daughters of Liberty. I know by now that the FBI is well aware of our previous work on behalf of the now dismantled Star Chamber. We have Charlotte Sadler as our prisoner who is well for the time being. For her safe return, the Sadler's will give us the sum of five-million dollars that will be left at a location we will provide at a later date. The bills are to be in denominations no greater than fifty dollars. You have seven days to get the money."

Joey felt there was no need to redo the tape. It was short, sweet and to the point. By the next day all of the mainstream media, the Sadler's, and the FBI would have plenty to work on. He and his SDL group could just sit back and watch everyone run around like decapitated chickens.

Lomax called Jeannie at home early Tuesday morning. "The hostage-takers have made a move," he said, sharing that several media outlets had received letters and the finger prints on the paper belonged to Charlotte Sadler. Also, a tape had been received by the Sadler's. Lomax asked her to get to the Sadler residence as soon as possible. Jeannie called Ismail and said she would pick him up on the way.

"There's something familiar to how things are playing out, but I can't put my finger on it," Jeannie said to Ismail. "Why the extra communication with all the news agencies? The tape to the Sadler's should be enough. I think we're being played somehow."

The male voice on the tape had no distinct accent, nor was there any background noise. The speaker identified himself as the leader of the SDL. Jeannie looked at Ismail, and the look they shared was that this had to be Joseph Alan Rogers, aka Joey. "How much do you think five-million dollars would weigh?" she asked Ismail.

"Gee, let's see, Ismail said, pulling out his iPhone. One million dollars in one-hundred dollar denominations would equate to twenty-two pounds per million, or one-hundred ten pounds for five million. If it's in twenty dollar bills, that would be one-hundred ten point twenty-three pounds per million, or over five-hundred and fifty pounds. You know what?" Ismail remarked as Jeannie smiled. "If we make the ransom in ten-dollar bills, they would have to contend with over one-thousand, one-hundred pounds." Even if they pay in twenties, it still can't be carried in a suitcase. How the hell do they expect to grab the loot and run?" Ismail asked.

"Like I said, something doesn't add up. I could see them requesting that the money be sent electronically to an offshore account, but to physically try to move five-million dollars doesn't make sense, and Joey is very intelligent. Remember what Judge Baldwin said about him. No, he has already made these calculations."

Rap music was directed toward the closet all day long. Charlotte tried to cover her ears but was only partially successful. Nighttime finally brought relief when Joey shut it off and opened the door. He pulled out the stinking bucket of urine, re-shut the door, and took it to the bathroom where he flushed it down the toilet. Without rinsing the container, he returned to the closet and placed it inside. He asked if she were hungry or thirsty? She said, "Both."

Joey returned with a bowl of cereal and a bottle of water. "Here you go," he said, again shutting the door. At 10 p.m. he told Chico, "She's all yours." Chico opened the door and Charlotte scooted as far back into the depth of the closet as she could. Chico shut the door and began taking his clothes off. "Take yours off, or I'll do it for you," he said. Charlotte began to cry, but did as she was told. She could barely breathe with Chico on top of her, relief coming only when he had finished and stood to put his clothes back on. Charlotte curled herself into a ball and fell asleep.

Chapter
Twenty-three

On the sixth day, the phone monitored by the FBI at the Sadler's estate rang. "This is the SDL. By now you should have the money available for delivery. Tomorrow at nine a.m., you'll make the drop. We want you to place the money inside a U-Haul truck and park it in front of Abe's bookstore on Telegraph Avenue, Berkeley, next to the mailbox. Don't try any tricks like placing an agent or two in the back of the truck. They will be killed. If we see any other pigs in the area, Charlotte will be killed. Once we have the money, we'll give you directions for finding her."

Jeannie had the two monitoring agents send the recorded phone call to Darcy who prepared for everyone to listen to it in the briefing room. Jeannie had requested that Pinheiro come to the bureau with her that day and offer suggestions, although he already told Jeannie that kidnapping cases were not his specialty. The voice had been that of Joey again.

"I still don't get it," Jeannie said to the assembled group which included the SAC. "How in the hell do they think they'll get away? Walk up to the truck and drive off with the money? Even if we were out of the immediate area, they'd have to think we would bug the truck, and if you noticed, the only thing they gave us was a specific time and location for the drop. What is that all about?"

"I agree," said Ismail. "Something smells. They have something else up their sleeves. Maybe it's a decoy, but a decoy for what?"

"What if they have no intention of picking up the money?" Pinheiro said, looking at everyone. "Instead they're just screwing with us. Jeannie already told me about the actual weight of so much money. I think it's a charade. They're trying to pull your chain."

"Regardless, we have to go along with their request. What else can we do? Let's follow the procedures for a ransom drop. Stakeout the area, put agents inside some of the shops, and have trailing cars on parallel streets," said the SAC.

Jeannie left the group and walked to Darcy's office. "There's something I want you to do for me as quickly as you can."

"What's that?" Darcy asked.

"I want you to get as much information as you can about SLA, the Symbionese Liberation Army. I need you to do a presentation for the team."

"You mean the Patty Hearst case?" she asked.

"Exactly. There are too many similarities between that old case and this one. I remember studying it when I was going through behavioral analysis training at Quantico. This whole thing stinks and Joey seems to always be one step ahead of us. Maybe if we review the SLA and their crimes, we can get ahead of him. Let me know when you have it put together and you can present it to all of us."

Jeannie reviewed her thought process with SAC Lomax. He stated that he had also thought about the similarities being played out, and how Joey seemed to be following patterns similar to that of the SLA.

Jeannie, Ismail, and Pinheiro went to their favorite IHOP and agreed to not talk shop in the hope they could clear their minds. Talk involved the Super Bowl trip, and then the Russian history lesson Pinheiro received at the NSA briefing. "Jesus!" said Ismail. "You're placed in a small room with your wife, daughters and son, thinking you're going to have your photograph taken, and the next thing you know, an assassination squad enters and kills everyone. I can't even imagine the carnage, screams, blood and smoke in that room. Even those asshole gunmen must have panicked when the bullets ricochet off the girl's bodies."

"Yeah, and then after they recovered, their greed took over and they were down on their hands and knees picking up gems mixed with blood and human remains," Pinheiro said. "Strange times."

Jeannie's cell vibrated, and she answered. She looked at Ricky and Ismail and told them that Darcy completed the task she had requested. They needed to get back to the briefing room. Ismail paid their bill, stating it was the least he could do for his cousin getting Super Bowl tickets to see the Chiefs beat the 49ers. Jeannie just gave him a push while saying thanks to Ricky.

When the three arrived back at the bureau, they joined SAC Lomax and several other members of Jeannie's team as well as Darcy and Burk in the large briefing room. The front white-board was illumined with photos of eight individuals--four males and four females. Sitting at a table, Darcy waited until she got the nod from Jeannie to start her presentation. First, Jeannie addressed everyone, stating again that the whole investigation seemed similar to an older event that took place in the bay area. She told those assembled that she had asked Darcy to do some research and wanted her to share what she found. She then nodded, and Darcy began her presentation.

Darcy identified the eight photos as Emily Harris, Willie Wolfe, Donald De Freeze, Bill Harris, Camilla Hall, Patricia Hearst, Angela Atwood, and Nancy Ling Perry. Under the photos were the letters SLA, and in parenthesis, "Symbionese Liberation Army." "These were the members of the infamous SLA who, on February 4, 1974, kidnapped Patty Hearst shown here in the photo with her nickname, Tania. They were, in short, a band of domestic terrorists.

"The leader of the group was this man, Donald De Freeze, and ex-con. DeFreeze was the SLA's only black member. His seven-headed SLA hydra-like cobra symbol was based on the seven principles of Kwanzaa, with each head representing a principle. I won't go into that since I don't think it's relevant at this stage. Anyway, The SLA formed as a result of prison visitation programs of the radical left-wing group Venceremos Organization, and a group known as the Black Cultural Association in Soledad prison.

"The SLA formed after Donald DeFreeze, alias General Field Marshal Cinque, escaped from prison. He'd been serving five years to life for robbing a prostitute. DeFreeze took the name Cinque from the leader of the slave rebellion which took over the slave ship Amistad in 1839. DeFreeze escaped from Soledad State Prison on March 5, 1973 by walking away while on work duty in a boiler room located outside the perimeter fence.

"DeFreeze had been accused by some sources as an informant from 1967 to 1969 for the Public Disorder Intelligence Unit of the Los Angeles Police Department. DeFreeze had been active in the Black Cultural Association while at the California Medical Facility, a state prison facility in Vacaville, California, where he made contacts with Venceremos members. He sought refuge among these contacts and ended up at a commune known as Peking House in the San Francisco Bay Area. Venceremos associates and future SLA members Willie Wolfe and Russell Little, and arranged for DeFreeze to move in with their associate, Patricia Michelle Soltysik, in the relative anonymity of Concord, California. DeFreeze and Soltysik became lovers and began to outline plans for founding the Symbionese Nation.

"On November 6, 1973 in Oakland, California, two members of the SLA killed school superintendent Marcus Foster and badly wounded his deputy, Robert Blackburn, as the two men left an Oakland school board meeting. The hollow-point bullets used to kill Foster had been packed with cyanide."

"Hold on a minute, Darcy," said Jeannie. "Only a few of you in the room received word that upon autopsy of Charlotte's limo driver, a hollow-point bullet was removed with traces of cyanide." The room filled with soft whispers. "Sorry, Darcy. Go ahead."

Darcy nodded and continued. "Although Foster had been the first black school superintendent in the history of Oakland, the SLA condemned him for his supposed plan to introduce identification cards into Oakland schools, calling him a fascist. In fact, Foster had opposed the use of identification cards in his schools, and his plan was a watered-down version of other similar proposals.

"On January 10, 1974, Joseph Remiro and Russell Little were arrested and charged with Foster's murder, and initially both men were convicted of murder. Both men received sentences of life imprisonment. Seven years later, on June 5, 1981, Little's conviction was overturned by the California Court of Appeal, and he was later acquitted in a retrial in Monterey County. Remiro remained incarcerated in San Quentin State Prison, serving a life sentence.

"Little later stated that the one who actually pulled the trigger that killed Foster was Mizmoon Soltysik. Nancy Ling Perry was supposed to shoot Blackburn, but she botched it and DeFreeze ended up shooting him with a shotgun.

"In response to the Remiro and Little arrests, the SLA began planning their next action--the kidnapping of an important figure to negotiate the release of their imprisoned members. Documents found by us at one of the abandoned safe houses revealed that an action was planned for the full moon of January 17. The FBI didn't take any precautions, and the SLA didn't act until a month later.

"On February 4, 1974, publishing heiress Patricia Hearst, a sophomore at the University of California at Berkeley was kidnapped from her Berkeley residence," Darcy continued, as she displayed a picture of Patty Hearst on the whiteboard. "Around nine o'clock in the evening there was a knock on their apartment door in Berkeley, California, and a group of men and women with guns drawn burst in. They grabbed a surprised nineteen-year-old college student named

Patty Hearst who had just gotten out of a shower and was only wearing a towel. Her fiancé, Steven Weed was beaten up and left on the floor of their apartment. They threw Patty Hearst in the trunk of their car and drove off.

"Why'd they snatch Hearst? To get the country's attention, primarily. Hearst was from a wealthy, powerful family. Her grandfather was the newspaper magnate William Randolph Hearst. The SLA's plan worked and worked well. The kidnapping stunned the country and made front-page national news.

"But the SLA had more plans for Patty Hearst. Soon after her disappearance, the SLA began releasing audiotapes demanding millions of dollars in food donations in exchange for her release. At the same time, they began abusing and brainwashing their captive, hoping to turn this young heiress from the highest reaches of society into a poster child for their coming revolution.

"On April 3, the SLA released a tape with Hearst saying that she'd joined their fight to free the oppressed and had even assumed a new name. A dozen days later, she was spotted on bank surveillance cameras wielding an assault weapon during an SLA bank robbery, barking orders to bystanders and providing cover for her confederates.

"The SLA issued an ultimatum to the Hearst family. They would release Patty in exchange for the freedom of Remiro and Little. When such an arrangement proved impossible, the SLA demanded a ransom in the form of a food distribution program. The value of food to be distributed fluctuated. On February 23 the demand was for four-million dollars and peaked at four-hundred million. Although free food was distributed, the operation was halted when violence erupted at one of the four distribution points. The crowds were much greater than expected, and people were injured as panicked workers threw boxes of food off moving trucks into the crowd.

"After the SLA demanded that a community coalition called the Western Addition Project Area Committee be put in charge of the food distribution, one-hundred thousand bags of groceries were handed out at sixteen locations across four counties between February 26 and the end of March.

"The FBI was conducting an unsuccessful search, and the SLA took refuge in a number of safe houses. Hearst later claimed she was subjected to a series of ordeals while in SLA captivity that her mother later described as brainwashing. The change in Hearst's politics has been attributed to Stockholm Syndrome, something I'm sure we're all aware of. It's a psychological response in which a hostage exhibits apparent loyalty to the abductor.

"The SLA subjected Hearst to indoctrination in SLA ideology. In Hearst's taped recordings, used to announce demands and conditions, Hearst can first be heard extemporaneously expressing SLA ideology on day thirteen of her capture. With each successive taped communiqué, Hearst voiced increasing support for the aims of the SLA. She eventually denounced her former life, her parents, and fiancé. She later claimed that at that point, when the SLA had ostensibly given her the option of being released or joining the SLA, she had believed she would be killed if she turned them down. She began using the nom de guerre Tania, after Che Guevara's associate, Tania the Guerilla.

"The SLA's next action was to rob the Hibernia Bank branch at 1450 Noriega Street, San Francisco, during which two civilians were shot. At ten a.m. on April 15, 1974, SLA members burst into the bank, including Hearst holding a rifle, and the security camera footage of Hearst became an iconic image. She has denied willing involvement in the robbery in her book, Every Secret Thing. The group was able to get away with over ten-thousand dollars.

"The SLA believed that its future depended on its ability to acquire new members and realized that because of the killing of Marcus Foster, few if any people in the Bay Area underground wished to join them. Cinque suggested moving the organization to his former neighborhood in Los Angeles where he had friends whom they might recruit. However, they had difficulty becoming established in the new area. The SLA relied on commandeering housing and supplies in Los Angeles, and thus alienated the people who were ensuring their secrecy and protection. At that stage, the imprisoned SLA member Russell Little said he believed the SLA had entirely lost sight of its goals and had entered into a confrontation with the police rather than a political dialogue with the public.

"On May 16, 1974, Teko and Yolanda, also known as William and Emily Harris, entered Mel's Sporting Goods Store in the Los Angeles suburb of Inglewood, California, to shop for supplies. While Yolanda made purchases, Teko on a whim decided to shoplift a bandolier. When a security guard confronted him, Teko brandished a revolver. The guard knocked the gun out of his hand and placed a handcuff on William's left wrist. Hearst, on armed lookout from the group's van across the street, began shooting up the store's overhead sign. Everyone in the store but the Harrises took cover, and the Harrises fled the store and drove off with Hearst.

"As a result of the SLA's botched shoplifting incident, the police acquired the address of the safe house from a parking ticket in the glove box of the van, which had been abandoned. The rest of the SLA fled the safe house when they saw the events on the news.

"The next day, an anonymous phone call to the LAPD stated that several heavily armed people were staying at the caller's daughter's house. That afternoon, more than four-hundred LAPD officers along with the FBI, LASD, CHP, and LAFD surrounded the neighborhood. The leader of a SWAT team used a bullhorn and announced, and I quote, occupants of 1466 East 54th Street, this is the Los Angeles Police Department speaking. Come out with your hands up. A young child walked out with an older man. The man stated that no one else was in the house, but the child intervened, stating that several people were in the house with guns and ammo belts. After several more attempts to get others in the house to leave, a member of the SWAT team fired tear gas projectiles into the house. This was answered by heavy bursts of automatic gunfire, and a violent gun battle began. The police fired semi-automatic AR-15 and AR-180 rifles. The SLA members were armed with M1 Carbines that had been converted to fully automatic fire. Police also reported that the SLA had created homemade grenades from 35mm film canisters and had thrown them at responding officers."

"Hey, I remember that shoot out. It was on every news station at the time according to my Dad," Burke said. "The damn press and liberal media started questioning the need for so much firepower by the police, if you could believe it," he added.

"I could go on," Darcy continued. "But suffice it to say, everyone in the house died that day either from bullet wounds or fire. When the fire department went through the debris the next day, it was learned that neither Patty Hearst nor the Harris's were inside the house. As a result of the siege, the remaining SLA members returned to the relative safety of the San

Francisco Bay Area and protection of student radical households. At this time, a number of new members gravitated towards the SLA. The active participants at this time were Bill and Emily Harris, Patty Hearst, and a few others.

"On April 21, 1975, the remaining members of the SLA robbed the Crocker National Bank in Carmichael, California. During the robbery, bank customer Myrna Lee Opsahl, a forty-two year-old mother of four children, was killed when Emily Harris discharged the shotgun she was holding, apparently by accident. Five SLA members were ultimately held accountable for the murder and robbery, but not until almost twenty-seven years later, in early 2002.

"Patricia Hearst, after a long and highly publicized search, was captured on September 18, 1975, along with the Harris's and two others, all rounded up in a San Francisco safe house." Darcy turned to Jeannie indicating the she was through.

No one spoke in the room for a few seconds. Jeannie looked at Lomax who looked at Pinheiro. "Wow," said one of Jeannie's new replacement agents. "I had never heard of the SLA or the big shootout in LA."

"Hey, with the way education is today, I believe you," Ismail said, smiling. He looked at Jeannie as if to say, "Well boss, what's next?" She did not disappoint.

"Thank you, Darcy. That was a lot of work to be completed in such a short time. I owe you."

Looking at the group, Jeannie was about to speak when Lomax took the floor. "Well, it seems to me that Joey and the SDL are trying to mimic the old SLA from the seventies. You have the cyanide bullet used on the limo driver, the kidnapping of Charlotte, and now the request for ransom versus food distribution for her release. Sadly, I imagine that if Joey is going down this path, poor Charlotte is being indoctrinated as I speak, and probably worse."

"Morning everyone," Joey said as he entered the kitchen with Amy in tow. "By tomorrow the feds will have already parked the U-Haul truck with or without the fifty-million dollars. Knowing we're serious and out of concern for Charlotte, I'm sure they'll use real bills. We need to watch out for tracking devices on the money and inside the bags. They'll probably have agents in many of the Telegraph Avenue shops, and undoubtedly the truck will be bugged. Surveillance mobilized units will be on side streets and everyone will be waiting for our next move. Payday, ladies and gentlemen, is tomorrow.

"But for tonight we continue our brainwashing of little Miss Charlotte. Give her another month and she should break, maybe sooner. We'll continue to fuck with the FBI, but they'll never get close to us. Vicki, tonight you and Sandi will introduce yourselves to Charlotte. Make it as sweet and as sensuous as you can, not like Chico last night," Joey said as he laughed and punched Chico on his arm.

Chapter
Twenty-four

The truck with the ransom money was under surveillance from 7 a.m. until 4 p.m. Jeannie opted for the money to be in $10 denominations, forcing the suspects to deal with the weight estimated at over 1,100 pounds. No one approached the truck. The only activity was a store owner calling the Berkeley Police Department, complaining about a large U-Haul blocking potential customers from seeing his shop. Jeannie called off the surveillance and told an agent to return the U-Haul to Chase Bank where the money would be offloaded.

"You were right," Jeannie said to Ricky who riding with her in the bureau car. "They were just pulling our chain. The problem with this case as I see it, is that no one can get a handle on Joey and the SDL's motivation. Sure, greed's part of it, but with the money and stuff they took from Pavlenko's residence, including the Romanoff jewelry, hell, they could've split to a country that doesn't allow extradition. Instead, they kidnap an heiress and play ransom games.

"Yeah, he's loosely following the old SLA playbook. But like you, I can't figure out his end game. Now we have to wait for their next move," Ricky said. "Like Lomax said today, poor Charlotte."

"OK everyone, let's call it a night," Jeannie announced through her radio. She and Ricky planned to follow the U-Haul truck back to the bank, making sure the ransom money was secure. A bureau car drove up next to the truck and an agent got out and climbed into the cab, but quickly got out and signaled to Jeannie and the other units close by to join him. "I don't like this," Jeannie said.

"Yeah, something's wrong," said Pinheiro.

The agent opened the truck's back rollup door and everyone froze. They stared into an empty space with the exception of a neatly cut square in the floor bottom. "Fuck!" Jeannie said as she had Ricky and the other agent helped her up into the truck. With a flashlight in one hand and her weapon in the other, she advanced toward the hole in the floor. Peering down she saw a manhole cover slid off to the side and a large cardboard box that had been used to both shield removal of the cover and sawing the hole in the truck bed. "Shit, shit, shit!" she said as she stomped around the back of the empty truck space. "God damn it! Why didn't I think about that?" No one said anything. Jeannie focused her flashlight into the tunnel and slowly climbed down into the blackness, her flashlight guiding her way to the bottom. Once there, she saw several Radio Flyer wagons, the kind children play with, lined up neatly in a row. Taped to one of the wagon handles was a note made of cut newspaper letters that read, "Thank you. Let's do business again real soon."

"Damn, that couldn't have gone down any sweeter," Chico said. "I can just see the FBI's faces when they open the back of the truck and see it empty."

"Great plan, Joey," said Vicki.

Joey stood over the sacks of money lying on the safe house floor. "Thank you. I have to admit Billy, that when you were under the truck cutting away I was worried that smoke, sparks, or something would tip them off, but that sawblade worked as you said it would. OK, for a job well done, I think it's time to get some food, booze, drugs, and get merry. What do you all say?"

Amy and Sandi went on a food run and returned with pizza, KFC, and even Chinese food. Billy, still on an adrenaline rush, bought beer and hard liquor with Chico in tow. While they were away, Joey got rid of some of his adrenaline rush by having rough sex with Amy who enjoyed it.

After dinner and a little partying, Vicki and Sandi had their way with Charlotte in the closet. When they finished, Joey brought in the tape recorder with a script for Charlotte to read. By this time, Charlotte did not try to cover her naked body. The brainwashing was taking place, Joey thought. With her breasts fully exposed she started reading the communique into the mic. With the taping complete, Joey removed the cassette, wrapped it in a brown paper bag, wrote the address of a large San Francisco newspaper outlet on it and handed it to Chico. "You know what mailbox to use to mail this, right?" he asked. Chico nodded, took the small package and headed out the door.

Two days later while Pinheiro and Jeannie were driving across the Dumbarton Bridge to the bureau, her cellphone went off. The screen displayed SAC Lomax's name. "This is Jeannie. We're on the bridge and on our way in. What's going on?" she asked.

"We just got another communique from the SDL and Charlotte. Looks like she's starting to turn," Lomax said.

"Shit! OK, depending on traffic, we should be there within the hour." Jeannie said and then disconnected. Glancing toward Ricky, she continued, "Another tape recording, and Lomax said it appears the Stockholm syndrome is happening."

At first, all that was heard on the tape was a hiss, then a female began speaking. "This is Tania. Charlotte is no more. I denounce my social elite parents and what they stand for. I am embarrassed after learning that my father amassed his wealth off the sweat and blood of foreign workers for the almighty dollar. His workers are forced to work sixteen-hour days for two dollars, while he and his alcoholic wife hobnob with celebrities and social parasites. You wine and dine with your liberal Democratic friends who prey on the weak, saying they care for them, but only to secure their votes during elections. I now have a better loving family. I am no longer treated as a prisoner but as a fellow soldier of the SDL. The silent majority has only recently awakened, but they need to be shown the path to correction, to get back to the rule of common sense. We will show you the way."

Pinheiro, Ismail, Lomax, Jeannie, Darcy, and Burk filled the room with silence. Finally, Darcy turned off the recorder. "OK, let's follow procedure. Darcy, Burke, get the cassette down to fingerprinting and then do your normal search for background noise, etcetera. I'm sure we'll come up empty, but maybe they've made a mistake," Jeannie said.

"Sounds like more SLA shit to me," Ismail quipped. "Maybe Charlotte has turned, or just maybe she read what they wanted her to say."

"What about her reference bit about the silent majority who only recently awakened, but need to be shown the path to correction, to get back to the rule of common sense?" Jeannie asked.

"Yeah, I caught that too," replied Pinheiro. "They're not asking for a new ransom drop. Besides Charlotte, saying that she's not a prisoner, but a member of the SDL, what else of substance was there on the tape?"

"Only what you and Jeannie pointed out," Lomax said. Ismail just nodded. "OK, everyone's worn out from this investigation. I'm ordering everyone to take off early and to try clearing your minds by doing something else. I'll see everyone here tomorrow morning at nine." With that command, Lomax left the briefing room.

"Hey, works for me. I don't need the door to hit me in the ass. I'll see everyone tomorrow," Ismail remarked as he left the briefing room and headed toward the parking garage.

Jeannie told her secretary to inform Burke and Darcy that they were to go home early per the SAC's orders, and that she would see both of them in the morning at 9:00 a.m. She and Ricky grabbed their jackets from Jeannie's office and headed to the garage. "How about takeout tonight?" Ricky asked.

"Chinese?" Jeannie answered.

"Sounds good to me."

Once through the Dumbarton eastbound traffic, they stopped briefly at a local Safeway and each created a Chinese meal from the buffet. Neither had talked about the case while driving to Jeannie's house, but both had been mentally processing it.

"What do you want to drink?" Ricky asked as he laid plates and forks on the table near the Chinese takeout boxes in the kitchen.

"Diet Coke's OK with me," Jeannie replied. She took a seat opposite Ricky as he brought a glass filled with ice and a can of soda and sat down. Jeannie had already opened her plastic takeout food container and began eating her Orange Chicken. "You know, we both think Joey's pulling our strings, that there's another motive at play."

Ricky took a bite of his Wonton, and after swallowing said, "I thought your SAC said we weren't to discuss the investigation."

"Yeah, I know. But don't tell me you haven't been thinking about it the whole time since we left the bureau," she responded while placing a forkful of broccoli and beef in her mouth. Before he could answer, the doorbell rang. Jeannie looked at Ricky and they both got up and walked to the front door, both still wearing handguns. Jeannie looked through the peephole and silently mouthed to Ricky that it was Delores. Opening the door, Jeannie greeted Delores politely.

"Hi Jeannie. Boy, you're off early today," Delores said, extending a "Hi" to Ricky. "I just wanted to let you know that the film you told me about, you know, Last Ounce of Courage, it so inspired me that I took on the homeowner's association about their stupid rule on Christmas displays, and guess what? They backed down. Now we can display whatever we want. Isn't that great?" Jeannie responded that it was great news, but noticed that Delores saw the engagement ring on her figure. "OMG! OMG!, you got engaged. Oh, and to a looker I must add," as she looked at Ricky. " I'm so happy for you both. When's the wedding day?

"Well it just recently happened and we haven't even discussed a date yet," Jeannie said in reply.

"Oh, that is just great, just great! Well, I must be running along. Congratulations again. I need to get home and tell my hubby the good news. Bye," she said as she began walking briskly toward her house. So fast in fact, that one of her curlers fell out. She stooped down and grabbed it, and then continued her walk home, trying to reinsert the curler while losing one of her slippers, causing her to stop again.

Jeannie shut the door after watching Delores jog back to her house. "You're in trouble now, mister," she said, smiling at Ricky.

"What?" he asked.

Jeannie glanced at her wristwatch and said, "In about 40 minutes, everyone in the neighborhood will know that we're engaged.

"That fast, huh?" Ricky asked.

"Oh yeah," Jeannie said with a smile. "Delores is a one-women neighborhood alert."

Finishing dinner, Ricky said he wanted to take a hot shower since his back was a little stiff. "Riding in your Vette with those incredible seats, and then switching to your bureau car seats does a number on my back."

"Go ahead honey. I'll come up after I load the dishwasher."

"You know, if we decide to stay here after we marry, we might want to get a spa for the backyard," he said, walking upstairs.

"Oh, that would be so nice to come home to, wouldn't it?" Jeannie said.

"Oops. I just thought of something," Ricky said, stopping midway up the stairs.

"What's that?" Jeannie asked.

"I can see us in the spa with you getting frisky and sexy, and before we really get down and dirty, Delores looks over the fence in her curlers, asking us what we're doing."

"Oh my God, you're right. We might have to buy a gazebo for privacy," Jeannie said. "That might work, but she might still hear you during climax and have a heart attack," Ricky said as he hurriedly headed up to the bedroom.

"Very funny, very funny," said Jeannie. "You'd better run."

After cleaning up the kitchen, Jeannie remembered that Ricky did not have a chance to share his thoughts about the case before being interrupted by Delores. Hearing the shower run, she went into the second bedroom where she had her whiteboard covered with items pertaining to the case. She reached into her pocket and pulled out a piece of paper with notes she jotted down while listening to the tape recording and placed in on the white-board.

Included in her notes was the statement, "The silent majority has only recently awakened, but they need to be shown the path to correction--to get back to the rule of common sense. We will show you the way, " which she silently reread to herself. *"OK Joey, you little fuck, what are you trying to say here?"* she thought. She heard the shower being turned off and went to the master bedroom to grab nightclothes so she, too, could take a shower. Ricky came out of the bathroom followed by steam. He was wrapped in an oversized bath towel. "How do you feel now?" Jeannie asked.

"That's for you to tell me," he replied with a lustful look on his face.

"Give me fifteen minutes and I will," she said as she entered the bathroom and closed the door.

Around 4:00 a.m., Jeannie woke up after being inspired during one of her lighter sleep stages. *"I got you, you bastard,"* she thought as she slowly got out of bed, pulled on sweat bottoms and SF Giants long-sleeved shirt, and walked in the darkness to the second bedroom. She closed the door, and while looking at the spiderweb design on her board she saw references to the SLA, the SDL, the Star Chamber, arson, the Romanoff jewelry, Pavlenko's home invasion, Charlotte, the ransom plot, and the tape recordings.

She began moving items around the board as she remembered them in her dream.

She did not hear Ricky enter the room since she was now on a roll. He coughed and brought her back to reality. "Hi babe," she said as she gave him a quick kiss.

"Looks like you've been busy," Ricky said.

"Uh-huh," she replied.

"I'll bring you some coffee," he said, but he did not think she heard him or realize he had left the room. He returned with two steaming cups of coffee and handed one to her. A sip of the hot liquid appeared to bring her back to the present.

"I'm sorry," she said, giving him another kiss. "I think I found something that might help us. By the way, Delores interrupted you from telling me what your thoughts were about the investigation."

Ricky took a sip and looked at the items rearranged on the board. "Well, it looks like you are way ahead of me. Why don't you go first?"

Without further prodding, Jeannie went to the white-board. "OK, as you can see I've moved things around, and, here is my reasoning. Tell me what you think.

"Joey was the head of the Sons and Daughters of Liberty, right?" Before Ricky could agree, Jeannie continued. "He worked for the secret court, the Star Chamber, arranging for assassins to carry out the court's verdicts. To do so, you have to conclude that he felt the court's actions were justified and that he relished carrying out death sentences. OK, so here is Joey, a person who solidly believes in the red, white and blue, defended our nation, and leans more toward the Timothy McVeigh crowd than the liberal Democrats. Because of what happened to his mother and alcoholic father, he saw that some people are not judged by their actions. Therefore, he felt that through the Star Chamber he was an arm of the court, meting out justice. What do you think so far?" Jeannie asked.

"Makes perfect sense to me. Go on," he said.

"OK, things appear to be going along fine for the Star Chamber and the SDL until Judge Baldwin gets arrested for his involvement in child porn. That had to hurt Joey. Here was a justice of the Star Chamber, bringing justice to those that thought they were above the law, and low and behold, he learns that one of their own is a pervert. To make matters worse, the judge was even involved in the sex island escapades. As Joey processes these realizations, he finds out that several of his assassins were being killed on orders of the Star Chamber justices. That was the final straw for Joey and he decides to take matters into his own hands. How am I doing ace?" she asked.

"Not bad. I want to see what else your beautiful mind and body has put together," he replied, continuing to sip his coffee. Jeannie was too wired to sip more of hers.

"I don't know how Joey was introduced to Pavlenko, but based on what Ismail saw at the crime scene, he had a connection with the liberal billionaire. This was shown on the tapes when Joey was invited into the mansion without question. What I think, is that some of these anarchist activities, you know like the one that happened recently on the Berkeley campus, had to be funded by someone. That someone was Pavlenko. Joey, still having contact with remaining SDL members uses funds provided by Pavlenko, and there is our connection. During one of his visits, Joey must have seen the Romanoff jewelry, and later that prick's weapons arsenal. Joey needs funds, and he and the SDL hit Pavelenko's estate, and voila, he has money, the Romanoff gems, and guns galore." She then paused and finally took a sip of coffee that by then had cooled.

Jeannie winked at Ricky and said, "How does it feel?"

"Feels good. Please keep going while you're on a roll," he replied.

She took another sip, said it was good coffee and walked to the right side of the whiteboard. "OK, Joey seeks revenge from the Star Chamber for his comrades being killed on orders of the Star Chamber. The Star Chamber was attempting to clean up all of their loose ends after Judge Baldwin was arrested, including the Star Chamber's last known location. He started off by killing judges Katamoto and Swartz, but knocking them off one by one was too slow since he had other plans to execute. Somehow, he was able to convince the secretive court judges that he wasn't responsible for the Katamoto or Swartz killings, and convinced them to re-establish the Star Chamber." She stopped and looked at Ricky.

"That ties into the warehouse fire where the remaining judges were killed off," he said.

"That's my guess," she replied.

"So now he's gotten revenge for his compatriots and he decides to go after Charlotte, following a script left behind by the Symbionese Liberation Army i.e., the kidnapping of Patty Hearst," said Ricky. "But what about the ransom?"

"I think it's all a ruse. Remember the original ransom demand? Millions and millions of dollars. None of us could conceive of how they could move that much money based on the currency's weight. It was as if he read our minds. He never planned on taking the truck, and that's why he told us to park it at a specific location. He knew that if we parked the U-Haul by the mailbox, it would be right over the man-hole cover. I know this is way out there, but what if Charlotte is now more of a liability than an asset. You said you couldn't figure out why he wanted to kidnap Charlotte when he already had all that cash from Pavlenko's mansion, not to mention the Romanoff jewels. It's simply to brainwash her. He wants to make her part of the SDL."

"That makes sense since there haven't been more ransom demands." Ricky said, still looking at the board while walking toward it. "So, what the fuck is he up to?" he asked.

Jeannie stood next to Ricky with a now empty coffee. "Listen to this interesting part of Charlotte's recording, a section I wrote down. She said, or read, that the silent majority has only recently awakened, but they need to be shown the path to correction, to get back to the rule of common sense?"

"Yeah, I've been racking my brains all night long and can't come up with any concrete idea as to what this shit means," he said. He looked at Jeannie who had a huge grin on her face. "You've solved it?" he asked.

Chapter
Twenty-five

Tim was a seventeen-year-old who, unless you counted the many times he saw his sister in her panties and bra, never had anything close to a sexual experience until he met Connie, an inexperienced but inquisitive sixteen-year old neighbor. After ensuring his parents that he had completed his homework for the night, he met Connie at their prearranged meeting spot, normally behind a large tree across the street from what they thought was a vacant house. What would normally start out with French kissing, eventually culminated in an encounter with his hands under Connie's bra while she stroked his manhood until he came in her hand. On this occasion, both were oblivious to what was going on in the house across from them, especially him, since he was concentrating on Connie's hand on his penis.

A group hauling equipment into the vacant house across the street finally caught his attention. He saw at least five people, males and females whom he did not recognize, make several trips from a van into the house, carrying sleeping bags and what looked like Coleman lanterns, in addition to various other unidentifiable items. Soon an interior light appeared inside, but it was quickly blocked by someone placing a blanket over the window. Spending most of his time on porn sites and always changing channels when the news came on, he did not know much about the SDL nor the kidnapped Charlotte.

After a successful sexual encounter with Connie, he walked her home and returned to his house. He found his mom and dad watching Fox News. He got a bowl of ice cream and decided to sit down with his parents for a while. The news broadcast began with updated information about the SDL and a description of their crimes, then they showed photos of the group as well as Charlotte Sadler.

"Shit, shit, shit!" he said as he dropped his bowl of ice cream on the floor. His dad began yelling at him for the mess he made. Yelling to his parents he said, "I think those assholes just went into that abandoned house down the street." His parents began asking him for more specific details and after being convinced, his dad dialed the number on the screen. After misdialing, he called 9-1-1. He was so frantic that it took the dispatcher a few minutes to get all the details before advising the watch commander. While this was transpiring, Joey, Amy, and Charlotte left the residence.

Everyone was in the large briefing room, including SAC Lomax. Jeannie with Ricky's help had taken the items from the whiteboard at her house and had taped them to one of the walls in the briefing room. Darcy and Burke were the last to arrive, carrying bags of bagels and cream cheese. Seeing this, Jeannie told everyone to grab something to eat while she was rearranging the items. Ricky refilled both his and Jeannie's coffee cups, allowing her uninterrupted time to put everything up on the board that she felt was important. Finished, she turned to the now seated group.

"OK, early this morning Ricky and I had a brainstorming session. He and I formulated this, and by no means do we claim it's100% accurate."

"Get on with it. We'll tell you what we think," Lomax said, encouraging her.

Jeannie, outlining her contention in the same manner she did earlier with Ricky, explained the connections between events and people involving Joey and the SDL. Before getting to the information on the tape recording, she paused and asked for questions or criticism of her and Ricky's brainstorming and conclusions that far. Ismail was the first to speak, saying it all made sense and that they had laid out a convincing story that any jury should be able to follow. Lomax expressed his concurrence with Ismail. Burke and Darcy remained silent.

Jeannie began again, "OK, here's where we may have some disagreement. In the last recorded communique from Charlotte, she made the following statement, and I quote—reading-- The silent majority has only recently awakened, but they need to be shown the path to correction, to get back to the rule of common sense? End of quote. Here's what I think this is referring to. Remember, Charlotte is simply reading verbiage given to her by Joey. It's coming from him. The silent majority he's referring to started with the election of President Trump. A person running on the platform of not being a politician and certainly not being part of the swamp in Washington D.C. Remember all of the campaign speeches by candidate Trump condemning the liberal left and all of that politically correct crap. The silent majority elected this non-politician who began the arduous task of draining the swamp.

"Joey, I feel, believes that this coincided with the work of the Star Chamber and the SDL. Make people accountable for their actions. No one is above the law. In other words, a return back to common sense. Now, here's the scary part. As I said earlier, I don't think the kidnapping of Charlotte is really the endgame. No, I think this last part alludes to what's to come. When Joey says, but they need to be shown the path to correction--to get back to the rule of common sense,

Joey has a bigger plan. He plans on his group showing the silent majority a better, quicker way, to eliminate those who don't stand for his principles." Jeannie stopped and established eye contact with everyone in the room. No one spoke. An eerie silence invaded the room. A few took a sip of their drink, some placed a piece of bagel in their mouth, but no one said a thing.

Finally, the silence was broken by Lomax, saying that Jeannie's and Pinheiro's logic made perfect sense to him, but added that Joey and the SDL were still a step ahead of them, especially if he had already picked a target. "You're right Jeannie. This part is scary. We do not know what they will strike, when they will strike, and on what scale. All of their activities so far have been based in our area, but when the Star Chamber was in operation, they were international."

Chapter
Twenty-six

I n Jeannie's office, she, Ismail, and Pinheiro were racking their brains about possible targets Joey would be attracted to. The three found themselves in a similar situation when they were confronted with three separate jihadist teams sent to California. After identifying two of the targets and being able to prevent one from occurring, they had to continue guessing what the final target might be. Fortunately, Darcy and Burke were able to decipher a riddle by bin Laden, and with the aid of the U.S. Navy SEALS, they prevented the BART tube between San Francisco and Oakland from being blown up. In the present situation they had no clues or riddles to break. All they had was speculation.

Jeannie's' desk phone rang. It was her secretary. "Jeannie, the SAC needs to see you asap in his office. If you know where agent Flores and Pinheiro are, he wants them there too." The three quickly made their way down the hallway to Lomax's office. Upon their arrival, he told them that the Concord Police Department had a vacant house under surveillance. They received information that a teenager had seen the SDL hiding in it.

"How good is the information?" Ismail asked.

"They had an undercover unit pass by, and they saw a van in the driveway and a car parked on the street. A records check found that the homeowner lived out of state. A call to that individual confirmed that no one should be in the house. They ran plates on both vehicles and they don't match. It's assumed they've been switched out. They're assembling their tactical team as well as the Contra Costa Sheriff's office, but said they would hold off making any contact until we arrive. Take as many agents and you need."

Jeannie told him she felt the three of them would suffice, and that would avoid a cluster of too many law enforcement agencies getting involved. He agreed and told them all to be safe. Opting to take Ismail's bureau car, they headed for the Bay Bridge. Traffic at that time of day was fairly light. It would be a few hours before commuters would start heading away from the city to the East Bay. Ismail switched his law enforcement radio over to the mutual aid channel, and the three began monitoring the situation from afar.

"You know, this reminds me of that SLA shootout in LA," Ismail said to no one in particular.

"Sure does," said Pinheiro from the backseat. "How do you want to do this, Jeannie?

"Well, we'll contact the commanding officer at the scene, and unless he or she requests specific help from us, it's their ballgame. They know the area, and it's their SWAT team that'll be involved, not ours," she replied.

One hour later, they arrived two blocks away from the house where the command post had been set up. Jeannie contacted Captain Lisa Walker of the Concord Police Department who was inside the Contra Costa Sheriff's Department's large Emergency Response Vehicle. With the addition of Ismail and Pinheiro, the large vehicle was somewhat cramped. Following introductions, Captain Walker pointed to a large area map with the vacant house under surveillance circled. She pointed out the location of their spotters, sniper units, and uniformed officers.

Nearby neighbors on both sides of the street and to the rear had been evacuated as silently and as quickly as possible. Jeannie told Captain Walker and the SWAT officers in the ERV that if it was the SDL in the house, they would have firepower that would make everyone envious. Ismail listed the types of rifles taken from Pavlenko's house and provided a guess as to how much ammo they might have. Everyone turned and looked at Captain Walker and the SWAT commander. "OK, Jim. Get your SWAT officers as close as possible to the house." Looking at the two uniformed sergeants from the Concord Police Department, she told them to back up SWAT, pointing on the map where they should be stationed. "The FBI and I will be here at this angle from the house. Once everyone's in place, I'll call the people inside and let them know of our presence." She grabbed the large silver bullhorn off of the table that held the detailed operation map and said, "Let's go."

As they exited the ERV, Ismail leaned close to Jeannie and whispered, "How many officers do you think are involved in this operation?"

"I have no clue," she said. "I think we need to stick together and not get in their way." "Roger that," Ismail replied, looking at both Jeannie and his cousin.

As Captain Walker was announcing police presence, portable high-power lights simultaneously turned on and focused on the house. "To those in the house. This is the Concord Police Department. We want everyone to come outside with your hands in the air. I repeat, this is the Concord Police Department. The house is surrounded by SWAT officers. Come out of the house with your hands in the air." For about twenty seconds there was no response from inside the house. Captain Walker looked at Jeannie. Jeannie suggested that she repeat the same broadcast, but this time refer to Joey and the SDL specifically. Walker nodded and picked up the bullhorn, but before she could speak, all hell broke loose. Bullets began peppering neighborhood vehicles on the street that belonged to the evacuated. Windows were being blown out. Some of the firepower coming from the house was automatic, indicating that Joey and the SDL had modified some of the weapons. SWAT returned fire. Shots were exchanged for almost five minutes until the SWAT commander gave the order to fire tear gas canisters into the structure.

Jeannie and her team could see tear gas filling the house and exiting through broken windows, yet the intense firepower continued. A blanket that had covered the front window caught on fire, adding to the smoke coming from the house. SWAT officers at the rear and sides of the house were also taking rounds. The fire seemed to be spreading inside the structure as more windows exploded either from intense heat of from rounds fired through them. A short time later, smoke began pouring out of the roof vents.

Jeannie stated that for anyone to survive that long in the house, they had to be using gas masks. Walker agreed. The shooting continued as the fire found its way to the roof. "How could they still be firing?" Walker asked Jeannie.

"They're in the crawl-space under the house," Pinheiro said.

Using binoculars, Walker focused on the house's foundation and said that Pinheiro was correct. That was where the shots were being fired. "All units, the suspects are under the house. Focus on those locations."

It seemed that after Walker's announcement, the exchange of firepower increased.

Suddenly, a person covered in a burning blanket exited the house and began running in Jeannie, Walker, Ismail, and Pinheiro's direction, shooting an automatic weapon. Bang, bang, bang, bang came shots in rapid succession, bullets striking the sides and windows of Jeannie and her team's vehicle. SWAT returned fire, and quickly the aggressor was on the ground with the burning blanket.

Walker heard a scream and turned to see Jeannie on her knees next to Pinheiro. Ismail turned and saw that his cousin had taken a hit. Blood was coming from his neck and the right side of his chest under his vest. Jeannie applied pressure to the neck wound as Ismail tried to get leverage under the vest to do the same. "We need paramedics Code 3," Jeannie screamed. Walker noted that the gunman had been neutralized and called for the Paramedics to approach from a specified location away from stray bullets. Gunfire from the house stopped, as did returning fire. The structure was fully engulfed in flames, and the fire department made no effort to stop it since the structure was starting to collapse into itself.

Paramedics arrived and had to forcible remove Jeannie and Ismail to care for Pinheiro who was unconscious. Jeannie watched as they took his vitals and inserted an IV into his arm. As they placed him on a gurney and strapped him in, Jeannie told Ismail that

she would be going with the paramedics and to call
the SAC and fill him in. Jeannie asked the paramedics
what hospital they would be taking Ricky to and gave
that location to Ismail. She followed Pinheiro into the
ambulance and held his hand, talking to him as the
paramedic continued to apply trauma aid based on
instructions received from the hospital staff via radio.

Chapter
Twenty-seven

The Concord Fire Department and Contra Costa fire marshal investigated the charred Concord house remains. Three bodies were recovered from the crawlspace. The person who had exited the structure in a blanket and was shot dead on the lawn was identified as a woman. Her charred remains had been taken by the Contra Costa Coroner's office the night of the shooting. The bodies removed from the crawlspace the following morning were burned beyond recognition. It would take DNA analysis several days to determine that the bodies were that of Billy, Chico, Vicki, and Sandi. Vicki was the one who came rushing out of the residence in a blanket. None of the bodies appeared to be Joey, his girlfriend Amy, nor Charlotte. The search for the fugitives continued.

Two days later, Patrolwoman Alice Bettencourt was on routine patrol in the Haight Ashbury district of San Francisco. Her attention fell on a rear license plate attached to a faded blue Honda Civic being driven by a woman with a male in the passenger seat. The license plate was dangling from a clothes hanger used to attach it to the vehicle. After several attempts to read the waving license plate, she was able to gather the total plate number and called it in to Wants and Warrants. Dispatch notified her that there were no wants or warrants on a 2010 Dodge Caravan. She notified dispatch that the plates were on the wrong vehicle and that she would be making a vehicle stop near the next intersection. Before she could activate her lights and turn on her siren, the vehicle of interest came to a sudden halt. A female driver quickly jumped out of the vehicle with a handgun and fired three rounds at the officer, shattering the patrol car's windshield. Slamming on her brakes and taking a barricade position behind her open driver's door, Bettencourt began returning fire. Her first-round hit the female in the mouth, snapping her head back. The second round hit center mass and the female fell to the ground. Bettencourt did not notice that a male passenger had jumped out the vehicle and ran into a side alley, escaping the scene.

As support units with sirens blaring approached the scene, Bettencourt remained with her gun focused on the vehicle and body on the street. When backup arrived, they cautiously approached the vehicle. Bettencourt bent down over the female gunman and checked her pulse after kicking the handgun a distance away. She found no pulse. Still experiencing some temporary hearing loss from the shoot-out and the associated adrenaline rush, she thought she heard a female crying in the back seat of the Honda. She stood up, pointed her weapon at the vehicle and continued her approach. Positive the crying was coming from the rear seat, she pointed her weapon in that direction and told the individual to sit up and show her hands.

"Don't shoot, don't shoot," said a female who slowly sat up in the backseat. "I'm Tania, I mean, I'm Charlotte. Please don't shoot." Bettencourt, seeing other units arriving at the scene and drawing their weapons, told them to hold. There was a female in the backseat. She ordered the female to put both hands outside the rolled down rear window and then to slowly, with one hand, open the door. The door opened. "Please don't shoot me," the female said again.

"Come out slowly, showing your hands at all times," Bettencourt commanded. The female complied.

Bettencourt instantly recognized that it was Charlotte who stood facing her. Bettencourt told her to place her hands behind her head and interlace her fingers. "I don't have a weapon. Please don't shoot me," Charlotte said again. Suddenly, Charlotte urinated in her blue jeans, with urine collecting at her feet. Bettencourt ordered her to the ground and a second officer cuffed the teenager.

"Who was in the car with you?" Bettencourt asked. "Amy and Joey. Amy was the driver," she answered. On her radio, Officer Bettencourt indicated that one female was down, another was in custody, and the fleeing Joey's last known location. The message went to all units in the area. Joey could not be found.

The Sadler's used all of their political clout to gain their daughter's release, but to no avail. Although she had not participated in any crimes, law enforcement still needed to gather as much information as possible from her in an attempt to locate Joey. Late that evening after a marathon interview, the district attorneys of Contra Costa County and federal prosecutors released Charlotte. Should Joey be captured, she would be required to retell her story in court. Her nightmare was not over.

As firefighter Alex Mendoza stirred the dying embers of the vacant house to make sure no hots spots would flare up, he found a metal box. He pulled it from the debris and opened it. As soon as he saw the contents, he called his battalion chief, Anthony Stewart, over and showed him the box and the jewelry inside. "Wow," Stewart said, "We need to get the Sheriff's department over here."

The jewelry found its way to the Department of Homeland Security and the FBI. The President was advised of the event during his morning briefing and decided with his aides that a photo op was warranted. The following week, Lomax and Ismail were sitting in the Oval Office with the President. "I understand that Agent Loomis is at the bedside of DHS Agent Pinheiro. Please tell her that he is in the prayers of both me and the First Lady," said the President as the door to the Oval Office opened. Everyone focused on Vasili Sokalov from the Russian State Department as he entered the room followed by several film teams from the big media stations with Fox News front and center. On the President's desk was the chard metal box.

The President stood and walked around his desk to shake hands with Sokalov. While the cameras rolled, the President opened the box displaying the stolen Romanoff jewelry to both Sokalov and the media. After a few minutes, he handed the box to Sokalov saying, "I hope this can bring some sort of closure for your country and the remaining relatives of Czar Nicholas II."

After a long flight home to Mother Russia the next day, Sokalov met with his supervisor showing him the returned jewelry items. "Putin wants to also hold a press conference similar to the American President and show off the Romanoff pieces. He will put all the items, including these, on display."

The alarm went off in the segregation section of the federal maximum-security area. Officers ran to the area and found cell 321 open. As they got closer, they saw Officer Lake trying to remove a shirt wrapped around the neck of Baldwin who was lying on the floor near his bed, his head swaying back and forth in concert with Lake's movements. Baldwin's tongue was partially extended and his eyes were open. "He's gone," said Lake as he looked at the other office entering the room and several standing outside the cell. A sergeant arrived and went through all the motions. No pulse, cold to the touch. Baldwin had been dead for a while.

Concurrent investigations by the Correctional Department and the FBI found that the on duty officer whose job was to conduct security checks on Baldwin since he was a suicide risk, had falsified his reports to cover the time frame and that he had been sleeping on the job. In addition, the cameras pointed at the cell and hallways had malfunctioned and provided no information. The Correctional Officers Union refused to have all officers on duty polygraphed, feeding conspiracy theorists with new blood.

"Shalom," said Joey as he shook hands with the bomb maker who supplied the bombs that ended the lives of the Star Chamber judges.

"Shalom," was the reply. "I hope you were pleased with the results of my supplies."

"Very much so," said Joey. "It was because of your product that I came to seek you out again."

"Come, let us have some tea." They entered his garage and Joey took a seat opposite his host. After pouring each a cup of tea, Joey was asked what product he was looking for. Joey told him that he again wished to purchase several blocks of explosives similar to those used to eliminate the Star Chamber, but that this time, he needed something special.

"What do you request, my brother?" the host asked.

Joey pulled a small piece of paper with writing on out of his pocket and handed it to his host. The host looked at it and said, "What you request will be very hard to obtain. It is kept in a Level Four containment area due to its deadliness. Are you sure you want this?" Before Joey could respond, the host continued, "This item is a thousand times if not more deadly than the recent Corona-virus pandemic. There is no treatment for this. None. And, even if I could obtain this, how will you disperse it?" His eyes returned to the piece of paper.

"I realize how hard it might be to collect the amount I'll need to carry out my plan, but I'll pay you very well for your procurement. But, not only do I need this in these quantities, I also need for you to find a qualified expert who can weaponize it as an aerosol, and I need it by the date on the bottom of the paper." He pulled a large envelope from his back pocket and handed it to his host. "Here, my brother, is one-hundred thousand dollars to get started. Once you've obtained the material, let me know and I'll pay you what you and the chemist are due for your efforts." Joey then stood and was about to shake hands with his host, but his host raised his right hand and said, I need to request one thing myself, brother."

"What is that?" Joey asked.

"I want to know where my family and I should be when this is released."

"Not a problem" and with that Joey left without shaking hands. The host sat back down, poured himself more tea and again focused on the paper he was holding.

Jeannie had been staying at the hospital almost non-stop with only occasional breaks given by Ismail so she could go to a cheap motel, take a shower, and get some food and rest. Rest did not come easy nor did she have an appetite, but her body needed something to survive. Early the next morning she was back by Ricky's side, relieving Ismail. After an hour, Jeannie went down to the cafeteria to get a cup of coffee. She gave Ricky a kiss on his forehead before leaving the room. He had been placed in an induced coma shortly after arriving at the ICU.

She refilled her cup and began walking back to Ricky's room. A female doctor approached Ricky's room at the same time. Jeannie quickly approached the doctor and asked, "How is he doing?"

"Let's sit down," the doctor said in a fashion that alerted Jeannie it would be bad news. They walked to the waiting room area and took seats. "He's a fighter, but we need to go back in and see where he's bleeding. His blood pressure is very weak and he flatlined last night, but we got him back." Ismail had not told Jeannie that when she relieved him.

"Doctor," Jeannie said wiping tears and mascara from her cheeks. "Is he going to make it?"

"Right now, the best I can say is that he has a fifty-fifty chance," came the reply.